THE
FLIP
SIDE
OF
LIFE

JAMES E. MARTIN

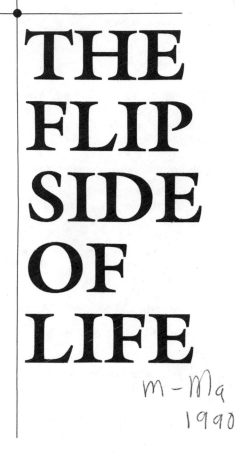

THE FLIP SIDE OF LIFE

m–Ma
1990

G. P. PUTNAM'S SONS
New York

1

G. P. Putnam's Sons
Publishers Since 1838
200 Madison Avenue
New York, NY 10016

Library of Congress Cataloging-in-Publication Data

Martin, James E., date.
   The flip side of life / James E. Martin.
      p.   cm.
   I. Title.
   PS3563.A7243F5   1990   89-77148   CIP
   813'.54—dc20
   ISBN   0-399-13523-5

Printed in the United States of America

1 2   3   4   5   6   7   8   9   10

This book is printed on acid-free paper.
                              ∞

To Keith
a Big Leaguer always

I

"BE GENTLE WITH HER," Helen warned me ahead of time. "She's innocent and maybe a little too fragile."

With a buildup like that, I wondered if I should put chintz curtains in my office windows and set Pound Puppies on the ledges. Before I could get around to it, Gladys buzzed to tell me Monica Brodbeck had arrived. I got up from my desk and went out into the short corridor to greet her. She was standing in a reception area the size of an elevator car, outside the caged offices of Moe Glickman Bail Bonds. The reception area itself looks as if it had been built to guard the National Debt. On the other side of the steel mesh, Gladys Keego was presiding, guarded in turn by her attack-trained shepherd. Monica was taking it all in, her expression telling me our combined corporate headquarters were every bit as bad as she had expected to find in a building slated for demolition.

She saw me approaching on her side of the wire. "Are you—" she started, and then paused to gather strength to finish the sentence—"the detective?"

"That's me." I pointed down the corridor behind me to the door lettered with my name and business:

GILBERT DISBRO
INVESTIGATIONS

She read the sign, then tried to read me while I sized her up. Older than I had expected, closing in on thirty, she was five years ahead of me, a little late in life to be innocent and fragile. She was also taller than I had imagined but thin as a gawky teenager in a way that would never let her be mistaken for a fashion model. She wore a print summer dress with only straps across her bare freckled shoulders. Her colorless brown hair was drawn back tight, held by a barrette at the nape of her neck and then allowed to fall loose down her back without the hint of a curl. I decided the innocence came mostly from her brown eyes, which were magnified by the lenses of her oval glasses. If I'd been forced to peg her with any occupation, it would have been librarian.

"I have a problem to discuss with you," she announced.

Marriage troubles was my first guess, which I retracted when I looked at her left hand clutching her purse with a grip no mugger would ever break. No rings of any kind. "Would you like to step into my office?"

She gave the suggestion more thought than it deserved, finally deciding that a short stroll down the hall was no worse than nuclear fallout. I held my door for her and Monica stepped across the threshold as if she expected a trap door to open under her feet. When it didn't, she took one more step and paused to examine the room. It had a desk and chair in front of the window where an air conditioner labored with a wheeze symptomatic of emphysema, a pair of file cabinets, a map of Cleveland on one wall with my framed P.I. license, and a pair of chairs facing the desk. I tried looking at it with a stranger's eyes. Seedy but not threatening.

"If you're thinking it looks familiar," I said, "you're probably remembering my segment on 'Lifestyles of the Rich and Famous.' "

"Really?" The word escaped at the same instant she realized Robin Leach wouldn't set foot here. She snapped her teeth down as if she wanted to catch it before it got away.

I invited her to a seat and held one of the chairs while she settled onto the front two inches of it. "I'm not worth a damn until I've had my morning coffee. Care for some?"

"Decaf?"

"Not a chance."

She passed on the offer and I poured some from the pot that sat on Joe DiMaggio's coffee maker. My mug sported the WVIZ-TV logo on its side. Helen had insisted on sending in a contribution during the last fund drive. I carried the mug to my swivel chair behind the desk, under the slant of the ceiling, and set it on the corner as I settled into my seat.

"You're a—special friend—of Professor Scagnetti's," Monica blurted out.

I nodded. "We're living together."

She had as much trouble digesting that news as she had coming down the hall. "She's older than you."

"About twelve years." I fished in my pocket for a crumpled pack of Camels. "Helen said you were one of her students. Are you still in school?"

"Part-time. I'm a junior high teacher but I take classes at Cleveland State. You know—to keep up my certification. Professor Scagnetti is my advisor."

"So when you had a problem, you took it to her and she sent you to me."

"Who would have thought that an English prof would know a private detective?"

"We met when I was in her writing class," I said simply, finally getting my cigarette lit and reaching for the coffee mug. "Do you think you could tell me what your problem is?"

"Missing persons." She watched me smoke as if it were something she had never seen before. "You're able to find people, aren't you?"

"Sometimes, if they get careless about concealing themselves. Who's missing?"

"Alan—Professor Gault—and his son, Brandon. They aren't there any more."

I nodded sagely. "One of the major elements in a missing-persons case." Monica's expression told me this was not a subject for levity, so I added, "Since when?"

"At least since Friday. The last time I actually saw them was a week ago today, Wednesday."

I flicked ashes into my ashtray. "Professor Alan Gault. Would he be a relative of yours?"

"No." For some reason the suggestion made her look away and brought a tinge of red to her ears. "I took a class from him last fall at Cleveland State, and then later I started working for him."

"Some kind of graduate assistant?" I guessed.

"Not at all. While I was taking the course—it was 'Radical Political Thought in the United States'—Professor Gault advertised for a tutor for his son. It so happened I was looking for a way to supplement my income, so I applied and Professor Gault hired me. Ever since the first of the year, I've gone to his house every Monday, Wednesday, and Friday to tutor Brandon. Last Friday when I went there at the usual time, no one was home."

"Brandon has a learning disability?" I asked.

"Oh, no. He's very bright for an eight-year-old, but he missed a lot of school a year ago March when his mother died. Well, actually, she killed herself. Brandon found the body. You can imagine the trauma that would be for someone his age. Professor Gault was teaching at the University of Cincinnati then. He resigned, gave up his tenure, to come here so Brandon would get away from the environment where all the bad things had happened."

"Is Professor Gault teaching any summer classes?"

"No. This is his vacation."

"Then why isn't it possible that he went away on a trip somewhere? An ocean cruise or a visit to the Grand Canyon, see his relatives, look up his old colleagues?"

Monica had been shaking her head at each possibility I raised. She ended my speculation with a definite: "No. He wouldn't just take off without notifying someone. He's too organized for that. Besides, he specifically asked me to keep up with Brandon's studies through the summer so he will be caught up by the time school resumes in the fall. Then there is his work. He's not teaching but he has a grant to work on his project—a book, a biography of William Haywood. You've probably never heard of him."

"Big Bill Haywood? The union organizer for the Wobblies back around the First World War? The guy with one eye who skipped bail to Russia and died there? Whose ashes are buried in the Kremlin wall? Or is the professor writing about the Bill Haywood who used to play second base for the Cards?"

So I was showing off a little. It had the effect I had

been aiming for. It impressed her. "You were right the first time."

"Living with an English teacher has some advantages." I drained the last of the coffee out of my mug.

"Can you find them?" she blurted out with hope humming in her throat.

"Sure I can. But the question you have to answer is, are you willing to pay me to do it? I charge twenty dollars an hour, plus expenses. It doesn't take long to run my fees into real money."

"I am prepared to pay you." It was a declaration. "I have some money saved up."

"We can start with a five-hundred-dollar retainer."

"Very well." If the amount bothered her, she covered it well. She opened her purse and brought out her checkbook. "How should I make it out?"

"You really are concerned about finding someone who isn't related to you."

She had her pen poised over her checkbook, but she was watching me with her magnified eyes. It was a disconcerting look. "Why shouldn't I be concerned?"

"For one thing, there's a tax-supported bureaucracy to handle this sort of thing. It's called the police department. Have you tried them?"

"They weren't very helpful. They said Professor Gault is over twenty-one and free to come and go as he pleases. They said they only get involved with missing persons when it's a juvenile or a mental incompetent or a suspicion of foul play. I tried to convince them foul play must be involved, but they said they needed something more tangible than the mere fact he's not home. After I made a pest of myself, they suggested hiring a private investigator."

"Some of my best cases come as referrals from the police

department. Did the police check the morgue and hospitals for you?"

She nodded. "They at least went that far."

"So you know nothing too awful has happened. Why don't you save your money and wait? Professor Gault will probably return before long with an explanation. It might be a lame one, but at least you'll see that he's back and your bank account will be healthy."

"I can't." She stabbed herself in the chest with the pen. "In here I know something is wrong. That man and his son are alone in the world. They could disappear and there would be no one who would miss them for a long time, no one who would do anything about it—except me. It would be irresponsible of me not to at least ask about them. That poor little boy! I—I—" Behind her glasses, her eyes sparkled and her lower lip quivered until she caught it in her teeth.

"You're letting yourself get worked up over nothing." I got up and toted my coffee mug over to the machine for a refill.

"The point is I'm very disturbed." She pulled a Kleenex out of her purse and dabbed her eyes behind the glasses. "Five hundred dollars is small change compared to the worry of not knowing. I'd gladly pay that. If you won't help me, I'll find someone who will."

She was determined to fill out that check in someone's name. Better it should land in my bank account than Pinkerton's. Monica was putting her pen and checkbook and used Kleenex back in her purse as I returned to my seat, remembering Helen had sent her to me for help. I made a noise of disgust and said, "My conscience won't let me take five hundred dollars from you, but I'm willing to put a couple hours' work on the case to prove your worries are unfounded, if nothing else."

"Thank you! How—how—much do you need?"

"Make it a hundred." I opened my bottom desk drawer, which is really a file cabinet drawer, and took out one of my standard contract forms. I twirled it into my typewriter, filled in the necessary blanks, pulled it out of the carriage, and turned it for Monica to see. She read it and then signed it along with her check, which had her phone number and address printed on it—an apartment on Triskett. I tore off the carbon of the contract form and passed it to her. "That's your receipt."

"On television," she remarked, "detectives never make people sign a contract."

"They don't do a lot of the routine things that have to be done. Tell me about Alan Gault. What does he look like?"

She opened her purse once more, rummaged around and came up with a Polaroid snapshot, which she passed to me. I put it facedown on my blotter. "You describe him," I told her.

"He's forty-two years old with eyes that are sort of gray and very understanding. They match the gray in his hair and some of the gray in his beard. Did I mention he has a beard? And he's tall, though not as tall as you are, but as thin. He should eat more."

I turned the photo over and looked for the man she had described. The nearest I could come was an ascetic-looking bird with a brindle beard, dressed in a corduroy sports coat, a plaid shirt, and jeans. Instead of understanding eyes, his looked at the camera with protective hostility, eager to get this posing over. He had to be Alan Gault because the only other person in the photo was a tow-headed boy in a Little League uniform, wearing a fielder's glove on his right hand and standing a little better than elbow high to the man, about right for an eight-year-old. The photo looked as if it might have been taken near the diamond. Trees in the background had buds but no leaves. I raised my eyes to my client. "You took this?"

She nodded. "It was Brandon's first Little League game. He'd never played organized sports before, and he was so excited about his chance. He made me come and take his picture with his dad. That's another reason Professor Gault would never take Brandon away. It would mean missing his games."

I was still groping for facts that might explain Gault's disappearance to Monica's satisfaction. "Has there been any sudden change in Gault's life?"

"Not really." But Monica had something she wanted to bring up, if she could work it into the conversation. "I don't know if you would consider it a change, but it was rather sudden. His sister-in-law showed up unexpectedly at his house."

Holding my mug in both hands, I creaked back in my swivel chair. Tones in Monica's voice told me she wanted this subject pursued, even if she found it distasteful to broach. "His sister-in-law?"

"His late wife's sister. Arlene Hammond." When she spoke the name, Monica wore the same expression she'd had on when I lit my cigarette.

"Is that so unusual?"

"In this case it was. I happened to be there when she arrived, going over Brandon's lesson while Professor Gault worked on his notes. The doorbell rang and when Professor Gault answered it, he was shocked to see her standing there with a suitcase in her hand. 'Arlene! You're in Cleveland!' was what he said. It was plain he hadn't been expecting her. Outside there was a taxi just pulling away from the curb. After a moment, he let her in and introduced her to me. It was the first time I ever realized he had a sister-in-law. She is one of those cheap and flashy artistic types, possibly attractive to some men, but past her prime."

Somehow I had the image of a silent movie vamp bursting in on a blissful domestic scene. "Where did she come from?"

"Cincinnati, most recently. She had a job there with one of the local television stations, something behind the scenes advising the anchor people on wardrobe and makeup and such. She also spent time in Hollywood and New York. I hear she once posed for a magazine without any clothes on. That would have been many years ago, while she still had her figure."

Even at that early stage of the investigation, my instincts told me Arlene Hammond was a lead that would have to be pursued further. "What brought her here?"

"I don't know. I gather that Alan was not on good terms with his in-laws. They had some reservations after his wife killed herself. You can understand how they could let emotions cloud their judgment."

"They blamed him?"

"They thought he had been too involved in his work. If he had paid more attention to her, he would have recognized the signs and perhaps have prevented her suicide. One thing in Arlene's favor is that she didn't believe that. 'I never agreed with the rest of my relatives,' she told him. It's one of the few things I heard her say."

Sometimes the toughest part of detective work is figuring out exactly what the client is asking you to do. By this time, my premise was that Monica wanted assurance Gault had not run off with Arlene. "Where is she now?"

"Alan let her stay with him for a day or two. Then he found her an apartment—subletting it from another faculty member named Hrnailovich, who had gone off on a sabbatical."

"Have you talked to her since Gault disappeared?"

She looked down at the toe of her shoe. "Not hardly."

"Well." It was simply background noise, like elevator music, that I made to give the impression that I was thinking. "The first step would be a visit to the professor's home to make sure he hasn't come back, if nothing else. Maybe one of the neighbors saw something that will help. After that, I could see Arlene and then ask around the faculty in case he mentioned something there."

Monica nodded her approval to my game plan. "My car is in a parking lot downtown. Shall we meet at Alan's house in Cleveland Heights in a half hour?"

"You want to go with me?"

"I have nothing better to do."

Taking the client along is generally bad practice. If the client has the leisure to go along, what is the point of hiring a detective for the legwork? Besides, the presence of the client too often creates a bad emotional atmosphere that makes people reluctant to talk. Most of all, it lets the client see how easy the detective's job is and raises the question of what twenty dollars an hour is buying. In this case I was willing to make an exception because I didn't consider it a serious investigation. My only intention was to put in the minimum amount of work to justify my retainer and then knock off for the day.

"You're welcome to ride with me," I told her. When she hesitated, I added, "It would save gas and my driving record is clean."

Before we left the office, I turned off Mr. Coffee and advised Gladys that I would be out in the field.

2

IN A CAGED LOT behind Moe Glickman's office building on West Third Street sat my car. It's a gray four-door Chevrolet Caprice, a car you might have trouble finding in the parking lot when you leave the shopping mall, which is the whole idea. If you would ever give it any thought at all, you might decide it belongs to a salesman. The backseat holds two cardboard file boxes. One of them has a bunch of hanging file folders that contain the forms I'm likely to need in the course of my work. The other one is filled with phone books and city directories from all over Cuyahoga County. My two cameras—Polaroid and Pentax—hang by their straps down the back of the front seat from the headrest on the passenger side, usually covered by my raincoat, which I drape over them.

I unlocked the passenger door, moved my raincoat, and let Monica slide in, then went around to the driver's side and got behind the wheel. I drove only as far as the gate in the chain-link fence, where I had to get out and unlock it, drive through, and lock it again behind me. At last we were on West Fourth Street, heading for Superior.

Monica was twisted around in her seat, looking for something over her right shoulder. "Where are your seat belts?"

"I cut them out."

"Isn't that illegal?"

"Probably. But I had to pay for them when I didn't want them in the first place and never intended to use them. So now I'm rid of them." I flipped the air conditioner to high.

"You might at least have left them in your car out of consideration for your passengers."

"They passed a law trying to force me to wear them, and I don't like that. Want me to take you to your car?"

She gave it some thought but said nothing. We approached Public Square, where I circled around to Euclid Avenue. As we tooled along, she told me a little about herself. Raised in Mansfield, she had gone to Ohio State and applied for a teaching job in Cleveland because she wanted to make use of her talents serving an inner-city school. She had found one without any trouble.

Seeing she was not a native, I pointed out some of the sights we were passing—the place where John D. Rockefeller's town house had once stood, the home he used only on Sundays when he came in from his estate at Fairhill to attend services at the Baptist church and teach his Sunday School class. Monica, for all her close association with a history teacher, had never heard about that. Farther east, we passed through a long stretch with Third World ambience, home to many of Monica's students, beyond the Cleveland

Clinic complex to the corner of East 105th where Leslie Towne Hope had once sold newspapers.

"Who?"

"Bob Hope."

Next came the cultural center—Severance Hall, the Art Museum, the campus of Case Western Reserve, and the University Hospitals, which housed the coroner's office and morgue. I turned up Mayfield Road and ascended Murray Hill, the center of the Italian community and home base for the Mob in the days when Eliot Ness was Safety Director. At the top of the hill was Fairhill Cemetery—the back end of Rockefeller's estate—where Garfield is buried.

"The president," I explained, "not the cat."

"I know that." She tried to put resentment in her voice but she couldn't stifle a giggle. "You surprise me. You're really quite knowledgeable about Cleveland."

"I grew up in Old Brooklyn, a section on the other side of the river where the streets are named for German poets and there's a Lutheran church on every other corner. When I grew up, I was a cop for a couple years until I was laid off. I guess you pick this stuff up."

Monica directed me to turn downhill onto Coventry past its boutiques with Gucci, Pucci, and Eldridge Cleaver rubbing shoulders. We went uphill again while Monica watched for the cross street she wanted. We were approaching it the hard way. If Monica had been able to give me a better fix on the location of Gault's house, I would have gone out Carnegie and Cedar, but she was coming at it the only way she knew. I sensed that Monica could live someplace a long time and still know only the major routes.

Things really were different here in the affluent suburbs. In Cleveland, it had been a hot summer morning with an overhead haze, the kind of day a photographer would call

overcast bright. Out here, the sun etched a sharp contrast
between light and shade. We went down the side street
Monica chose until she pointed out Gault's house. It was a
stone-fronted Georgian design meant to last through a couple more decades of hard use. I went past it, whipped around
in someone's driveway, and came back to park in front of
Gault's place. Now that I had a better look, it appeared even
more massive than I had first thought. It could well have
been a branch library.

"Your academic friend lives well," I noted as I turned off
the motor and thus killed the air conditioning.

"Between the sale of his house in Cincinnati and his wife's
insurance, he had enough to afford a handsome down payment." Monica started to open the door on her side of the car
but stopped with the latch in her hand, her attention on the
front of Gault's house.

The door was recessed in a cavelike alcove, and across the
cave entrance was a heavy iron door that might have been
the relic of a medieval dungeon, symptomatic of urban para-
noia in the last quarter of the twentieth century. As I
watched, the cell door creaked open and someone stepped
out of the cave into the sunlight, then turned and locked the
cell door again. The person who did that was a woman,
black, wearing a blue jump suit and jogging shoes. She
started down the flagstone path to the sidewalk.

Monica finished opening the car door and stepped out,
waving. "Mrs. Young! Clarice!"

The black woman paused two steps short of the sidewalk
and waited for Monica to run over to her. I followed at my
own pace.

"Is Professor Gault in there?" Monica was asking as I drew
within hearing.

The black woman—Clarice Young, I deduced—paused

to look at me suspiciously. She might have been fifty, and from a distance she had appeared to be a large woman. Now I saw that she was shorter than I had imagined, her eyes level with the knot in my tie. The jump suit she wore had a name stitched over the breast: *North Coast Cleaning Service*. There was also a photo ID tag attached to her collar with an alligator clip.

"This is—a friend," Monica said lamely. "His name is Gil."

Clarice Young ran her eyes over me, taking in my unbuttoned collar and loose tie, my soiled and wrinkled seersucker suit. It should have gone to the cleaners three days ago, but I had been reluctant to part with it during a heat wave. Her expression informed me I looked to her like the wretched wreck of a white man in some South Sea island movie. Still watching me, she at last answered Monica's question: "Nobody's there."

"Have they been home?"

Clarice pried her eyes away from me and looked at Monica. "Have you seen them this week?"

"No," Monica confessed.

"It don't look like anything's been touched since last week, not even the boy's room. Nothing's out of place and that ain't natural. I dusted some, but I didn't do anything else. It didn't need it."

I said, "You didn't find a note from Professor Gault, anything like that, saying he had gone somewhere?"

She shook her head.

"Is his car here?"

"I never looked."

I left the two women standing there and followed the driveway to the back of the house. A detached garage, a scaled-down version of the house, was there. The blank overhead door was down, but there was a walk-in door on the side that had a pane of glass in its center. When my test proved it was locked, I peered through the glass. A power mower, a snow blower, rakes and shovels, a bare cement floor in the center with an oil stain. I returned to the women and reported the results.

Monica nodded in a kind of smug satisfaction. "What did I tell you? Clarice, you just have to let us into the house."

"I can't do that, Miss Brodbeck." Without my presence, Clarice might have been more agreeable.

"Something's wrong. You said so yourself. Please, Clarice. Professor Gault needs your help. He'd want you to do it."

That argument was almost enough to sway her by itself. I said, "You can come inside with us to make sure we don't take anything."

"Well—" Clarice reached a decision and pulled her key ring out of her pocket. "Seeing it's you." She trudged back up the S-curve of the flagstone walk to let us in.

Monica rushed ahead, knowing her way around, while I lagged behind with Clarice watching me. I wasn't going to get lint on my shoe without her seeing it. I stood in the hallway trying to get a feel for the place and not receiving any vibes. Even a glance from my unskilled eye told me the place reeked of good taste and the money to buy it. Everything in the rooms was in proportion in colors that blended perfectly. It was a spread from a magazine, a display window arrangement, a movie set. Which was exactly the problem. Unless the house Gault had occupied in Cincinnati had been an exact duplicate of this one, there should have been some dissonance, a piece of furniture that was off, a drape that didn't match the wallpaper, signs of wear and tear from an eight-year-old. No such thing. Meaning what? That Gault had bought an entire houseful of new furniture?

I walked through the downstairs, into a kitchen without any sign an egg had ever been fried there, and back to the entrance alcove. Mail had been piled on a table there. I turned to Clarice, who had been dogging each step. "You brought this in?"

She nodded. "The mailbox was stuffed full."

I looked at the return addresses—East Ohio Gas, Cleveland Electric Illuminating, Marathon, American Express, a professional journal, no personal messages. I made a neat stack of it and turned to find Monica coming down the stairs.

"Nothing I can find," she said.

"Let's go at it systematically." I started with the basement, part of which was a recreation room, part laundry room. The only remarkable thing was a chalk board on the recreation room side, which Monica soon explained.

"Brandon and I usually do his lessons down here."

I returned to the main floor, leading the parade, and went through it again trying to find some sign of human occupancy. Over the mantel was a portrait of a woman posed standing with her hands in the pockets of her tan pants, looking over her left shoulder and up. The artist had not flattered her, portraying her as a rather plain woman, a face without makeup and brown hair of no particular shade cut fairly short. She was wearing a beige blouse with the collar turned up in back. The most striking aspect of the portrait was its lack of color, flesh tones not far from the beige blouse. It had been done in oils, but the impression was of watercolors that bled into one another. Up close, I saw a metal tag screwed onto the frame with the legend: *Patricia Hammond Gault, 1953–1988*.

"Alan's late wife," Monica said behind me.

We moved on to the second floor. There were four bedrooms up here, the master bedroom stretching across most of the front of the house. The closet proved Gault had occupied it. He didn't have a lot of clothes, but the labels showed he favored Brooks Brothers. The one photo I had seen of him had shown him wearing a tan corduroy jacket, which was not there.

"What do you make of it?" Monica asked as if she expected my acute powers of observation to produce all sorts of brilliant deductions.

"Hard to say without knowing his whole wardrobe. There are no empty hangers, but if he packed up he might have taken them along. Do you know of anything missing?"

"I've never been in this room before," Monica confessed.

I directed my next question at Clarice. "Should there be suitcases in there?"

"I think so but—" She shrugged. "I cleaned the carpet and changed the bed. I never paid much attention to what's in the closet."

Nothing like a definite answer. I went next to the bedroom where Brandon slept, the furniture and wall decorations betraying its use by an eight-year-old. It struck me as being unnaturally neat. All the toys were stacked on shelves or put away in the toy box. While I stood in the doorway, Monica pushed past me and took a tour of the room. She pointed to a wall peg.

"Brandon's glove and his Little League cap are missing. He kept them there."

Clarice agreed. "If they went off somewhere, he'd take them with him."

Monica looked in Brandon's closet, then went through some drawers. "I don't see his Pete Rose shirt or his baseball pajamas."

"They weren't in the wash," Clarice confirmed.

"Then it looks like they packed up." I moved on to the

next bedroom, the guest room, which had all the personality of a motel room after the maid has made it up. I toyed with the idea that the last person to use this room had once posed as a centerfold. Before my fantasies ran amok, I gave it a cursory check and went across the hall to the bathroom. There were two mirrors, the lower one virtually touching the top of the sink so an eight-year-old could see his face. I opened the medicine cabinet to see what substances might have been used here. The only medicines were innocuous over-the-counter products with one exception—a bottle of Valium that had been prescribed for Alan Gault a year ago in March by a Cincinnati doctor named Fulton—take as needed, no refill. Out of an original fifty capsules, I estimated, thirty were left. The time element put it close to his wife's suicide, a bad period he had gone through without leaning heavily on chemicals.

The rest of the bathroom produced only more uncertainty. Soap, deodorant, and other typical cosmetics were there, but that didn't mean he couldn't have kept a set of things packed for travel. I couldn't find a razor, but Gault wore a beard, so maybe he had no use for one. There were two toothbrush holders, one adult and one child, each with two brushes in its four holes. That could be all Gault and Brandon had between them, or it could mean they had packed some.

On to the last bedroom, which had been converted to a den. He had set it up as an office, creating a desk by laying an unfinished door across two short file cabinets. Behind the desk was a table holding an IBM word processor with dual disk drives and two printers—one dot matrix, one letter quality. Shelves filled the walls, most holding books, while those nearest the desk held paper and supplies. There were two full-sized file cabinets in the room and a lectern holding an unabridged dictionary. All of it was anchored too securely to be transported on a short trip.

Monica went directly to one of the file cabinets. "Look at this." She took down a long, narrow file box sitting atop one of the cabinets and put it on the desk to raise the lid. It was only large enough to hold three-by-five index cards and dividers running within a couple inches of the back. I pulled a card at random from a section headed "Paterson Strike—1913." The card held notes relating to Haywood's speech at a rally in Madison Square Garden, printed with a felt-tip pen in the kind of penmanship taught in mechanical engineering courses.

"These are his notes for the book," Monica explained. "He wouldn't go away and leave them. It's his whole career, his most cherished possession."

Nearly as significant as Brandon's fielder's glove.

"If they went somewhere, Brandon had time to pack his glove but Gault didn't have time for his notes," I mused. "One seems to cancel out the other."

After putting some thought to it, Monica had a suggestion: "Could it be they didn't leave together? Could Alan have dropped Brandon off with someone—a baby-sitter—and then gone off by himself?"

"Who would that be?"

"His in-laws?" Even as she brought it up, Monica was shaking her head. "They live in Fort Wayne, Indiana. Anyway, they don't seem to be on the kind of terms for that."

"His sister-in-law, Arlene?"

"Would you leave a young boy in the care of someone like her? I don't think she would accept him."

I agreed with her on one point. I would have conceded that Gault might have dumped the kid, but it wouldn't have been in the centerfold's lap. My tentative guess was that Gault and Arlene were sprawled on a beach in the Bahamas, while Brandon was left with someone. My scenario didn't allow Gault much time to work on his notes. "Maybe Arlene can shed some light."

"I doubt that," Monica said icily.

"Still, I'll ask her. Before we do that, I'd better check with the neighbors."

We left Gault's house then, allowing Clarice to secure the place. I started knocking on doors. At that hour, the only answer I got on either side of Gault's house was a lot of deep-throated barking that seemed to be coming from dogs considerably larger than a Mexican hairless. Across the street my luck was better. The woman who answered the door was half of a retired couple who were home more often than not. She had not seen Gault around for a week, she realized only as I asked the questions, but she had not been concerned about it, knowing he was a teacher on summer vacation. She told me that Gault's son didn't have many playmates his age to choose from in the neighborhood but was friendly with the Millstein boy on the next block and often cut through her yard to get to the Millstein house.

I drove around the block to get there and parked in the driveway and rang the bell, which earned me nothing but the agitated barking of their dog.

"I never thought of it this way before," Monica remarked, looking around the neighborhood, "but these homes are really nothing more than oversized doghouses during the day."

"Dinner time would be best to find someone home." We got back in my car, and I drove downtown on Carnegie. On the way, I asked Monica where she had left her car.

"Why? Are you trying to get rid of me?"

"Yeah. I'm going to see Arlene next and I don't think having you along would make for a frank discussion."

Monica accepted it—sullenly, but with good grace.

I added, "Besides, I might get lucky and then you would cramp my style."

3

I DROPPED MONICA at the parking lot where she had left her car, promising I would call her at home later to bring her up to date on any developments. Then I headed for the west Shoreway and followed that past Edgewater Park until it ran out onto Clifton Boulevard. To my right along the Lake Erie shoreline was the Gold Coast, a line of posh high rises with swimming pools on the roof. The place I wanted was a few notches below that in the pecking order and a couple blocks inland, one of the older five-story brick buildings on Clifton.

With a gerbil scampering around my chest cavity, I walked under a canopy toward my rendezvous with a center-fold. In the mailbox alcove, I located the buzzer *Hrnailovich,* the faculty member from whom she was subletting the apartment, and punched the button. After a few seconds, I got an answer:

"Who is it?" Distortion in the speaker system kept me from determining anything about her voice.

"My name is Gilbert Disbro, but that won't mean anything to you." Then came the lie, "I studied under Professor Gault in Cincinnati."

"He isn't here."

"Do you know where I could find him? I'm only passing through Cleveland and no one seems to know where he's gone."

"What is this about?"

"Bill Haywood."

That lie was calculated to get me through the locked doors. Whatever the situation was with them, she wouldn't want to be responsible for keeping Gault from information about his work. Sure enough, the door buzzed and I pushed through. The elevator lifted me to the third floor where I found the Hrnailovich apartment, 3C. I knocked and the door opened.

Let the record show she was wearing clothes—a pair of jeans that probably cost more than my suit, and a T-shirt cut off to reveal a midriff that allowed nothing to be pinched. The way the T-shirt hung in front gave credence to the editorial judgment that had chosen to display her charms as Miss February, or whatever.

"Mr. Disbro?" She held out a hand for a businesslike shake.

"Good of you to see me." I took her hand, spiky with rings, and allowed myself to be pulled gently across the threshold.

She closed the door behind me and put her back to it, facing me. I elevated the level of my gaze and reached a firm chin, a set of high cheekbones, a pair of blue eyes, arched eyebrows, a head of frosted brown hair worn fairly short in a businesswoman's cut. Neither the gorgeous sex object I had envisioned nor the wreck Monica had described, she bore a family resemblance to the washed-out portrait of her sister I had seen but claimed the advantage of all the genetic characteristics. Somewhere in her late thirties, she maintained her figure and, without makeup, her attractive features. Like Pope said ahead of me, it wasn't the individual parts but the way they were put together.

She gestured generally toward the interior of the apartment, clanking bracelets on her wrist in the process. "Why don't you make yourself comfortable? I've become an awful sleepyhead since I've gone into temporary retirement. I hate to admit that I just had breakfast, but at least I have some coffee made. Care for some?"

I told her that would be a godsend. She directed me to a seat in a breakfast nook between the living room and the kitchen, only one of the table leaves up. I went to it while she stepped into the kitchen, a sight worth watching in her epidermically fitted jeans. She was much shorter than I would have expected, five-two perhaps, yet her generally slender shape made me think even now she was taller. Arlene returned with a mug and a Pyrex pot of coffee. She set the mug down in front of me, filled it, refilled her own already on the table, and returned the pot to the kitchen.

"Cream? Sugar?"

"Plain black." Habit made me start cataloguing the surroundings until I reminded myself that, because Arlene was subletting, there was probably nothing here characteristic of her. I hoped not. Whoever Hrnailovich was, he was probably a man—or a very butch lesbian. The furniture looked square and hard as church pews covered with vinyl. The curtains were venetian blinds and drapes that looked as if they were made of burlap. Pictures were paint-by-numbers models that probably did nothing but hide cracks.

"Awful, isn't it?" Arlene asked as she came back and sat down at right angles to me. "Alan arranged for me to sublet this place while the tenant is off on a summer cruise. He teaches accounting and business administration at Cleveland State. I think he furnished it from offices in businesses that have gone bankrupt."

She was right. It really was waiting-room furniture. "Looks like my bachelor pad before I got married." Arlene glanced at my left hand and I explained, "I'm not any more."

She nodded and plucked a cigarette from the pack of Virginia Slims on the table and lit it with a white Bic. "You mentioned Bill Haywood."

"I need someone who can tell me if some letters I found are authentic. I was hoping Professor Gault could take a look and say it is or isn't Haywood's handwriting."

"Well, he isn't here." Arlene blew smoke over her shoulder.

"I found out he's on vacation, but he's supposed to be around researching his book. Some people at the college suggested looking you up."

"But I don't know where he is, either." Arlene stabbed out her cigarette even though it was only half smoked. "I haven't seen him since sometime before the weekend. Honestly, when you rang my bell, I was thinking about calling the police. That's how worried I am."

Arlene had more in common with Monica than my client could have imagined. For the first time, I considered the possibility that I might have a real case on my hands. "Is there any reason why Professor Gault would disappear?"

"Several." She looked into her cup and failed to enlighten me further.

"I heard that his wife, your sister, died."

"Tricia was a suicide. Alan has been very depressed about that. The whole family avoids discussing it."

It was an invitation for me to butt out. If I accepted invitations like that, I wouldn't be much of an investigator. "Maybe, being on vacation, he simply wanted to get away by himself, be with his thoughts."

"Possible." Arlene's eyes met mine, telling me again I was treading on unwelcome ground. My eyes, in a test of wills, were saying I would find out. The contest had sexual connotations. She broke it off first. "You ask a lot of questions for a student."

"I admired Alan. He was the one who inspired me to study history. Maybe he wasn't like a father, more like an older brother. I was sorry he felt he had to run off to Cleveland—afterwards."

Chips flew off her skepticism. "Alan has that effect on women—people."

"I want to help."

"There's nothing to help with. If Alan prefers to be off by himself, it would be an invasion of privacy to disturb him."

"If you believe that, why were you thinking of calling the police?"

"Because I don't know what became of his son." Arlene pulled another cigarette from her pack but didn't get around to lighting it. "You don't want to hear about our family squabbles."

"I'm willing to listen. Sometimes talking about your troubles helps."

Arlene dropped her unlit cigarette, got up and went into the kitchen, returning with the coffee pot. "This could be a long session." It signaled a victory for me, but I wasn't sure if I were really the winner. She poured for both of us, returned the pot, and when she sat down again I lit her cigarette and one for myself. Ready.

"My parents are behind it," Arlene began. "Mom is a fundamentalist religious crank and Dad is a retired deputy sheriff, a right-winger from the old school with a bumper sticker that says *Support Your Right to Keep and Bear Arms.* Get the picture? The dark side of Norman Rockwell. Dad's not so bad at times if you can stomach all that conservative politics, but Mom lives for her religion instead of using religion for a guide in her life. None of that stuff stuck with me, very little of it with Tricia, though they both tried hard enough to beat it into us. As soon as I was old enough, I got away."

"To the middle of *Playboy.*" It slipped out, being never far from the front of my mind.

Arlene laughed, not the best thing she could do for her appearance. Lines appeared on her face—parentheses around the ends of her mouth and deltas at the outer corners of her eyes. "So someone told you that already." She shook her head. "I'm afraid I'm like Bill Veeck."

"I don't see much resemblance."

"Veeck spent a lifetime doing many good things for baseball, but everyone always remembers him as the man who sent a midget up to bat."

"Eddie Gaedel. No one ever knows what became of him."

"And I'll always be remembered as the woman who once posed nude. Well, the magazine wasn't *Playboy* but one of its lesser competitors, and I wasn't even the featured centerfold. At least the reports on the extent of my wardrobe are correct. It happened back in the days when Larry Flynt was operating out of Columbus. I did it to get money so I could head out to the West Coast to break into pictures. I also did it to shock my parents."

"Did it get you anywhere?" I asked.

Arlene got up to cross the room and adjust a stack of magazines on an end table. The magazines made the place look even more like a waiting room.

"Study some of those old black-and-white reruns in syndication. You might recognize me in the crowd scenes. I danced in the background on 'Ozzie and Harriet,' I had a small part on the 'Twilight Zone,' I posed with a black eye for a Tareyton ad. Darryl Zanuck never called, although I could give you reports on the sex habits of some other producers. If you have heard of my famous pose, you must already suspect the rest of it. Putting out to get ahead was an act of spite against my parents, proof that my life could be every bit as sinful as they predicted." Arlene stirred her coffee. "That was my style. Tricia's rebellion was—less overt. She went along with the program up to a point. She went to college, studied hard, became a teacher—in a public school, though, not in a Christian academy. The break came when she married Alan."

"Your parents didn't approve?"

She looked out a window. From the third floor, the view was obscured by the top branches of a tree three feet outside the pane.

"By their lights, she couldn't have made a worse choice. He makes a living with his mind, he doesn't go to church, he holds all kinds of liberal positions. Hell, he's even a registered Democrat. A few months after the wedding, they let Tricia know she was always welcome to visit as long as she didn't bring her husband along. When Brandon was born, they doted on their grandchild but they disapproved of the way he was being raised—never baptized, never sent to Sunday School, allowed too much freedom. They saw it as their mission to bring Christian principles into Brandon's life. Mom has a personal 800 number to God she calls to get her instructions."

Arlene paused as if she realized how much she was pouring out to me. "Jesus! Something about you makes people want to talk all day."

"Your parents must have taken it hard when Tricia killed herself."

"She went to hell to burn eternally. No two ways about it." She rubbed her fingertips over a painting of sailboats and a dock as if she were trying to scrape away the surface for a vision of hell.

"Why did she do it?"

"No one knows for sure." Arlene flicked ashes into a ceramic tray. "My best guess is that she had a mental breakdown. She always felt inadequate, and lately Alan's career has been on the rise. That only made her feel worse. She felt he was on a plane so far above her she could never match him. She felt snubbed by the faculty wives. She was getting pressure and criticism and a load of guilt from Mom and Dad. Understand, this is an educated guess. Tricia never confided in me, even though I was right there in Cincinnati at the time. Everyone was shocked to hear she hung herself in the basement; no one was surprised."

This time it was my turn to fetch the coffee pot. When I had poured for us both, I said, "You were some kind of media consultant in Cincinnati."

"Those who can, do. Those who can't, teach. Since my career never went anywhere, I was perfectly qualified to tell others how it's done." She shook her head at the irony of it all. "Anyway, I sold out my share of the business. It gave me enough money to coast for three years. Five, if I hold expenses down."

"That was soon after your sister's death."

"So there must be a connection, right? Maybe there is. Maybe Tricia killing herself made me realize life is too short to be wasted. Maybe I wanted to smell the roses along the way. Maybe I wanted to help save Alan."

"From what?"

"My folks." She put out her cigarette and leaned her elbows on the table, studying my face. "Have you ever heard of a man who goes by the name the Monk?"

I had to remind myself that I was posing as a grad student, not a P.I. "Didn't I read something about him once in the Sunday supplements? A de-programmer?"

"He used to be when it was trendy. Lately he's into tracking down missing children—which means he snatches them from a parent in one state and drags them back to their other parent. His real name is John Monk, and he operates out of Indianapolis."

Her facts were straight enough as far as they went. Being in approximately the same profession, I knew enough about his reputation to avoid any association with him. Aside from his name, his moniker came about partly because he wore wild hair and a beard like John the Baptist and partly because he always claimed, whatever the circumstances, he was essentially doing the Lord's work. Much of the time his abductions were in direct violation of a court order. No matter. God, not some domestic relations judge, was the final authority in deciding who should be in charge of the child's soul. Whenever there was a contest, the Monk always hired out to the parent who promised to raise the child in a wholesome Christian environment. Besides his directives from God, John Monk also listened to his legal advisors who kept him skating just inside the law's bounds. His usual ploy was making sure the parent was along to take the principal heat. In most cases, any charges that got filed named the parent and "unknown accomplices." The abducting parent was usually too grateful for the help that had been given to roll over on John Monk.

"What does he have to do with any of this?"

"My father knows him from his days on the sheriff's department. John Monk used to be a deputy, too, in Allen County. A few months ago Dad was threatening to hire him to get Brandon out of Alan's clutches. He and Mom didn't believe Alan was fit to raise Brandon. That's what I meant when I said I came here to protect Alan."

"Do you know for sure your dad hired the Monk?"

"Not the kind of proof you would take into a courtroom. Still, I'm satisfied. Last Monday Alan took me out to dinner. While we were eating I happened to notice a man across the room with long hair and a beard. Every time I glanced up his way, I caught him watching us. Later, we went to a movie, and I saw him again in the lobby. That could have been John Monk."

Or maybe some guy who just liked to look at her. All I said was, "Even if it was the Monk, what was he doing following you?"

"Making preparation for the kidnapping. What I'm afraid of is that they tried to take Brandon and Alan fought. They hit him over the head and dumped his body in a ditch somewhere."

It would have been comforting to laugh off her theory except that it fit the facts that I knew so far. It explained why Brandon had packed his valuables, while Gault did not. "The police could check this out for you. Why don't you call them?"

"I don't have enough facts to go on, only worries." She picked up her cup and carried it over to the sink to rinse it.

Arlene turned around and worked at a smile. "I'm probably worrying over nothing. And I have no right to unload on you. But thanks for listening."

"I still want to find Professor Gault for my own reasons, so I'll be asking around. If I learn anything, I'll let you know."

"I'd appreciate that, Gil." The tone of her voice implied she knew all kinds of ways to express her gratitude.

I got out of there before I was tempted to investigate.

4

IN THE GLOVE BOX of my car I keep a copy of Helen's schedule so I will know where to find her if I need to get hold of her during the day. I consulted it before I headed back into Cleveland on the Shoreway. Because my work keeps me moving around, it's usually difficult for Helen to reach me during the day but much easier for me to find her. Knowing her schedule allows me to say hello to her at odd moments. She claims surprise visits like that give her a lift. I know they work for me. With both of us skittish from previous marriages, we have never been able to agree on a permanent commitment, so these little bits of bonding are always precious. Sometimes I think that getting into another line of work might help me settle into a stable routine, which in

turn would stabilize our life. That feeling usually lasts until
the next case opens up.

When I passed Municipal Stadium, the time and tempera-
ture sign was proclaiming eighty-six degrees at 11:42. I
looped onto the Innerbelt and exited at Chester, coming out
of the freeway ravine onto the Cleveland State campus. I
parked in a visitor space and made my way to the English
department.

Helen's class in freshman composition had broken already, but she was busy with a few students who were
lingering to ask about the marks they had received on their
latest papers. Having been present when Helen had graded
this batch, I knew that the remarks she made with red ink
were far less caustic than her asides to me while she marked
them. I eased into the starkly modern classroom and leaned
against a cement block wall to watch.

She was behind her desk against the chalkboard, while the
students formed a semicircle. Seeing her again made my
innards squirm with equal portions of lust and appreciation
and awe for the fact that she had taken me for her lover. At
thirty-seven—roughly the same age as Arlene—she looked
at least half a dozen years younger and had a slender figure
that would be slow to show her years. Today she wore a blue
cotton dress that was nothing more than an elongated version of one of my Oxford cloth button-down shirts, cinched
at the waist with a belt in a way that demonstrated her curves
were where they were supposed to be. Above her dress her
dark hair, worn shoulder length, framed a face with classic
Italian features sculpted into high cheek bones and concave
cheeks. Her eyes, like two opened cans of 10W-30 motor oil,
watched her students warily.

"This poem doesn't make any sense," a female in ragged-
bottom jeans and a T-shirt was complaining. "It talks about

two lovers being like the points of a compass. It says one end travels and one end stays put for the other to return. But one end of a compass always points north. That means the other end always points south and they never meet."

A male student at her side had been bobbing his head in agreement. "This John Dunney don't have his shit together."

"John Donne," Helen corrected, pronouncing it "Dunn." "Can you think of any other kind of compass that might make better sense?"

The male shook his head without giving it any consideration, but the girl was a little faster. "Oh, yeah! The kind you use in math class to draw circles. The kind with two legs and one of them holds a pencil."

"And you can move the two parts closer together to make small circles or farther apart to make large ones," Helen went on. "The metal end stays put while the pencil travels."

"How come the poet didn't say what kinda compass he's talking about?" the male asked.

"Well, he describes it pretty thoroughly," Helen told him. "Try reading it again and see if it doesn't work better this time."

"The whole poem?"

The girl tugged his arm, urging him toward the door, leaving me alone with Helen.

When they were gone, Helen lit the cigarette she had been toying with and rolled her eyes. I said, "No one ever told you teaching here would be like Harvard."

"I know. Sometimes I wonder if the students who enroll here have the basic material."

"Like the ex-cops who sometimes take courses from you?"

"Especially the ex-cops." She started walking toward me, slapping the classroom door shut en route. When she reached me, she slid her arms over my shoulders and around my neck, pulling my lips to hers, pressing her breasts into my chest and grinding her pelvis against my hardening genitals. The kiss was soft and moving with lots of tongue action. A long time later—too soon for my taste—she pulled away and asked, "Other than that, did you have a reason for coming here?"

"Did I? Oh, yeah. The case you referred to me, Monica Brodbeck. She wants me to find one of your colleagues, Alan Gault."

"Anything to it?"

"Earlier this morning I was doubtful. Now I'm a little more worried."

"Really?"

"No one seems to know where Gault has gone. Now I'm finding some things in his background that would cause him to disappear unwillingly. I was hoping you could steer me to someone on the faculty who might know something."

"Gault hasn't been here long and he hasn't made many friends." She thought about it. "You might try Damon Herlihy. They share an office in the History department."

"Where is it?"

"Herlihy won't be there now, but I have a notion where to find him. Buy me lunch and I'll introduce you."

"Deal."

Helen gathered up her purse, bookbag, and attaché case and led me out of the lecture hall. We cut southwest across the campus, which always reminds me of a Soviet apartment complex, toward Euclid Avenue. Helen managed to hook a free hand in my elbow, and I took note of the reaction we rated from the people we passed. In two-thirds of the cases it was zilch. College students are too self-absorbed to pay attention to their surroundings, lost in their efforts to hurry to the next class. Half of the remainder gave us only a cursory glance that registered no surprise. I suppose I looked scruffy enough to be a graduate assistant. The other half, who must have recognized Helen as a faculty member if they didn't know her name, gave me an eye caress. We might have made an interesting couple—me with light wooly hair and mustache, Helen shorter with her dark good looks—Nordic and Mediterranean origins.

On Euclid Avenue we turned west toward Playhouse Square. Helen asked, "That poem the kids were discussing, 'A Valediction: Forbidding Mourning.' Are you familiar with it?"

"You had me read it a few weeks ago."

"I've always liked it but I've never analyzed why. Then it dawned on me. The central image of the compass describes our relationship, me anchored in one spot while you roam free within limits. It goes right down to our work. I'm stuck in the classroom while you traipse over the entire city. Yet we are connected no matter how much geography gets in the way."

"I guess so." Discussing the way we lived was unusual for us. We simply did things without analyzing why. I had moved in with her at the low ebb of my life—when I had been laid off from the police department and my wife had left me. I had been taking courses at Cleveland State, working toward my degree in political science in baby steps, and Helen had been one of my instructors. Without admitting it to myself, I had begun building toward making a pass at her.

When we went out for coffee after class to discuss topics for my next essay, she mentioned how my handwriting and typing errors hurt my grade. She suggested trying a word processor. I had to tell her I couldn't afford it any more than I could hire a typist, so she offered to let me use hers. At the Victorian house she had purchased with her divorce settlement, I found her working hard to restore it, and not making headway. I dropped hints that I could do the work. We bartered—I would help with the carpentry in exchange for learning to use the word processor. Even after the term ended, I kept working for her. Somewhere in there—the increments were so small I never could pinpoint the time—it became more than a business arrangement. Finally I took her in my arms and didn't get slapped. Later, when I was about to be evicted from my apartment, moving in with Helen was the natural step.

At a bar named Armand's, Helen stopped and pulled me inside. In any other neighborhood, the place would have had to stretch to reach nondescript. Because it was near a campus, it had become a quaint and trendy hangout. The floor was linoleum and the furnishings were wood much carved by visiting students who had left their initials as a memento of their passing through. The bar ran along one wall, booths along the opposite side, tables in the center, and a juke box at the rear facing a square of bare floor twice the size of a card table top that might have been for dancing had the spirit moved any customers to boogie. Helen went far enough to see into the rear booth nearest the jukebox. Whatever she saw there made her signal me to follow as she forged ahead.

"Ms. Scagnetti! Helen! How good to see you here!" The voice came from the booth, a male voice with a touch of orator in it. The back of the booth seat kept me from seeing the speaker until he stood up as much as the seat would allow. Even then I saw only the back of his head, hair mostly gray and thinning, and the shoulders of a polyester sport jacket in a loud plaid.

Helen greeted and added, "Damon, this is my friend, Gilbert Disbro."

By that time I had moved up to the side of the booth where Herlihy and I could see one another.

Unfair as it is to judge a man when he's squatting in a half-rise, I could tell Herlihy was not very tall. Fifty-five, probably, with a bulbous nose traversed by broken red lines as if Rand McNally had been sketching across it. His cheeks were rosy and his eyes, as colorless as distilled water, had turned rheumy. Supporting evidence for my conclusion was on the table—a forgotten cheeseburger and a glass with three swizzle sticks beside it. Herlihy was a drinking man.

"So you're the one!" Herlihy said as he took my hand. "You're the young stud who puts the sparkle in Helen's personality."

"Guilty," I confessed.

Herlihy glanced at Helen. "Forgive me, but your sex life is the subject of endless speculation among the faculty. Rumor has abounded that you have found yourself a young man despite all the middle-aged swains around here who would have gladly applied for the position. Yours truly included."

Helen accepted it with good-natured tolerance. "Do you mind if we join you?"

"My honor."

Helen and I slid into the seat across from him, while Herlihy signaled the waiter and quickly drained his glass. The menu was chalked on a blackboard behind the bar, plenty of space considering the range of their selections. When the waiter came, Helen settled for salad and cottage cheese. I took two chili dogs and an order of fries. Helen's drink was iced tea; mine, coffee; Herlihy's, another bourbon.

"Neither of you drinks?" Herlihy asked, betraying a drinker's suspicion of anyone who doesn't share his habit. "You're not reformed drunks or religious nuts?"

I shook my head. "I don't drink for the same reason I don't eat pizza. I don't like the taste of it going down, and I don't like the way it makes me feel afterwards."

Helen said, "I saw too much of it in my family when I was growing up."

"Yet you both smoke." That was not an overly shrewd observation considering that I was lighting Helen's cigarette while waiting my turn to use the Zippo on my own.

"Constantly," I said. "Another reason not to take up another expensive habit."

Herlihy shrugged, willing to concede that we were at least half sane. "Word has it, young man, that you are a private investigator."

I showed him the leather folder that holds my state ID card. Herlihy slipped on a pair of half glasses and studied it as if it were a document of great historical interest. "I'll be damned! I don't suppose your work is much like we read about, eh?"

"Depends on what you've been reading, I guess. Right now my business is just getting established. Most of the time I'm working for a bail bondsman tracking down suspects who have jumped bail."

"Not a lot of them are hiding out on campus, are they?"

"Not as a rule. Today I'm working on a missing-persons case that has roots here."

"A student?"

"The man who shares your office, Alan Gault."

Herlihy looked at Helen as if he were seeking confirmation for what I had said. Helen nodded. "Do you know where he is, Damon?"

"At home, I presume. Hell, he's on vacation."

"I heard he won a grant to work on his book. I understand he's supposed to be around, even if he isn't handling a teaching load—doing research in the library or working in his office."

"He's been around, no regular schedule," Herlihy conceded as our waiter came back with our food and drinks. "Who is so concerned about him?"

"His sister-in-law, for one." Helen and I spent some time with our food, while Herlihy sipped his drink, watching us. I swallowed a bit of my first chili dog and asked, "You wouldn't have any knowledge about a man asking for Gault? Medium height, squat, dark hair, and a beard?"

"No one like that." Herlihy's answer was positive, but his tone degenerated instantly. "Except for—no, he wasn't anything like the man you described."

"Who wasn't?"

"A student I had a brush with awhile back. It wouldn't have any connection."

"Tell me about it anyway."

Herlihy looked across the table at Helen and me, seeing we had both stopped eating. He shrugged and primed himself with a sip of his drink. "One day last week—Monday, I think—I walked into our office and surprised a man going through Alan's desk. Or that was my first impression. Later, it turned out the man in question had an excuse."

I finished off my first chili dog, wiped my mouth and reached for a french fry. "It would be interesting to know what that was."

"This student wasn't the man you described. He was the opposite in every way—clean-shaven, tall, and thin to the point of emaciation, as if he had just come through a long illness. My first impression was that he was a junkie from Prospect who had wandered onto the campus."

"How old?"

"Twenty, give or take." Herlihy fortified himself and saw the only way to avoid a lot of questions was to narrate the incident. "It was about this time of day, when I was off on my lunch hour. In fact, I was on my way to this very place when I remembered some papers I'd left in my office. I went back for them. I found the office door unlocked, even though I had thought I locked it when I left. I entered and there he was bent over Alan's desk. 'What is going on here?' I asked. The young man jerked around, startled, but once the initial shock wore off, he proved to be quite reasonable. He said he had come to the office looking for Gault and found the door unlocked, so he entered."

"Could that be?"

"It's possible I forgot to lock up. The student told me he was trying to figure out which of us used which desk and then find some paper and leave Alan a note."

"He was a student but he didn't have any kind of notebook with him?"

"I don't believe he did, now that you mention it."

"The note had to be on Gault's desk? He couldn't have stuck it in the door or slipped it underneath?"

"Some of the very questions I asked him. I was very suspicious and insisted on seeing his student card. He produced it and I copied down the information." Herlihy reached into his jacket pocket and produced a brown-covered notebook from Woolworth's. He found the page he wanted and showed it to me.

Herlihy's jerky script didn't make it an easy task, but I managed to decipher the name: Theodore Wyckoff, with an address on Fleet Avenue in Slavic Village. Herlihy had also dated the entry, last Monday, and noted the time: 12:15 PM. There was also a student number and other information of more interest to a computer than me, but I copied it down in my own notebook. "What came of all this?"

"Nothing. I had no way of knowing if this Wyckoff had taken anything from Alan's desk or if he might have a legitimate reason for being there. There was no sign of forced entry to the desk as far as I could determine, and Alan has always been too neat to leave anything of value in the open. All I could do was wait to see Alan, but he hasn't put in an appearance since then."

The incident might have been significant or it might have meant nothing. Right now it was the only lead I had to follow. Helen and I finished our meal with Herlihy, excusing ourselves to get her back to class. Instead, she took me to the administration building and had me wait in the outer office while she used her authority to pull the record of Theodore Wyckoff. We found a vacant desk there and studied it together.

There was not a long history on him. For the last two years, since leaving high school, Wyckoff had worked at a series of low-paying jobs—gas station attendant, auto mechanic. He had enrolled only at the start of this summer's session in the hope of acquiring enough education to better himself—not an unusual decision for Cleveland State students. His high school transcript showed he had graduated in Decatur, Indiana. His ID photo showed a gawky kid with a receding chin, a prominent Adam's apple, and mousy brown hair growing wild. Helen studied the basic freshman courses in which he had enrolled without finding any connection with Gault.

I found a Xerox machine and ran off copies of everything in his file before I returned the originals to Helen.

"So what does it all mean?" she asked.

"The last time I looked at a road map, Decatur was only about twenty miles from Fort Wayne, the home of Gault's in-laws. That's too much of a coincidence not to have some connection."

"But what?"

"That's what I'll be asking Wyckoff."

5

LEAVING THE Cleveland State campus, I returned to the Innerbelt south for a few stops before turning off east toward Slavic Village. Only a short time ago, this part of Cleveland was a breeding ground of Polish jokes, but in recent years the city had wised up to what a natural resource it is. Historical markers have gone up and storefronts have been refurbished in Middle-European styles. The residential side streets west of Broadway, basically the numbered streets in the sixties, have remained defiantly unblighted as the owners have struggled to keep their property up.

The address for Wyckoff turned out to be an apartment building that nearly filled its block, leaving enough room on the corner for a grocery store specializing in pirogies. There was no parking space out front. I went around the corner and turned into an alley running behind the building, finding there were spaces reserved for tenants, no more than half filled this time of day. I decided no one would bitch if I used one for a few minutes and parked there.

As I got out, I noticed one of the cars, an aged Mustang that might have been a classic if it had not been so pitted by time and patched with bondo. Its trunk stood open, showing two battered suitcases inside. Someone appeared to be about to leave on a trip or was just returning from one. The suitcases had name tags attached with tiny leather belts. In passing I flipped one of the tags faceup: *T. Wyckoff.*

From the parking area, a gate in the fence led into the tiny backyard that had not seen a lawn mower this month. The back of the apartment building had a wooden balcony on each of its three floors and a wooden stairway that Z'd its way down the face. The doors on each floor were left open in warm weather, the tenants having opted to risk criminal depredations rather than heat stroke. I entered at the ground floor and walked down the hall to the mailbox alcove at the front of the building. *Theo. Wyckoff* occupied 304. There was no elevator, so I climbed two flights to his apartment door.

I listened there, thought I might have heard something, and knocked on the paint-blistered wood. Inside there was a small crash as something fragile hit the floor, and maybe a gasp. Then total breath-held silence. I knocked again. "Ted? You in there?"

More silence.

No law has yet been written compelling you to answer a door because someone knocks on it, or to pick up a phone merely because it rings. For all I knew, Wyckoff was dodging bill collectors. I gave it one more try, listened, and went away as quietly as the floor would allow, exiting by the rear stairway.

Back at my car I studied the terrain. The wooden fence was high enough to keep the car from being seen, and anyway, Wyckoff's apartment had no windows looking out onto the back. Unless he had rushed down the hall to the back door to watch me leave, there was no way for Wyckoff to have seen who was knocking on his door. My quiet departure had been designed to prevent that. I got into my car, drove away, circled around to the alley again, and entered from the opposite end. Across the alley from Wyckoff's building was another parking area for tenants of the building facing the next street. I parked there, ran all my windows down, and shut off my motor, sacrificing my air-conditioning. I slid over to the passenger side and screwed myself around so I could look out the back window. My line of sight allowed me to see over the top of the fence to the third-floor balcony.

I waited.

Heat from the sun beating down on the car made it seem longer than it actually was, ten minutes tops. When someone emerged from the third floor, it was definitely not Wyckoff. It was a woman carrying a cardboard box with her purse balanced atop it. Holding the box before her, she descended the stairs and dropped out of sight below the top of the fence. The box she carried had kept me from seeing much of her except for part of her stringy blonde hair and enough of her body to see she wore a tank top and a pair of cut-off jeans.

A moment after she disappeared, the gate in the fence opened and she came through, juggling the box, the purse, and the gate. It was too much. The purse toppled and landed on the parking lot. "Shit!" she said distinctly. She put down

the box and hunkered down to scoop up the usual female
clutter from the crushed stone—compact, Kleenex, lipstick,
hairbrush, snub-nosed .38, aspirin, mini-pads for those light
days. Her eyes darting around the area—not able to see me
the way I was positioned—she scooped it all back into her
purse, picked up her purse, and dropped it through the
window of one of the parked cars.

Wyckoff's Mustang.

She went back for the box and resumed carrying it. From
my perspective, it looked as if the box were walking on a pair
of female legs, like dancing Old Golds in those old commercials. She toted the box to the rear of the Mustang and put it
in the trunk with the two suitcases. As soon as it was down,
she slammed the trunk lid shut and took another guilty look
around. Then she trotted to the driver's door of the Mustang, got in, and started the car. Instead of pulling away, she
sat there with the motor running, resting her forehead on
the steering wheel. After a bit of breath catching, she dug
into the purse beside her and came up with a cigarette. She
managed to get her lighter going on the third snick and
inhaled smoke as if it were nourishment. Only then did she
back out of the space and go off down the alley.

Decision time. I could follow the Mustang or I could go
back to the apartment. I decided the apartment would stay
put, while it might be wise to know where the Mustang went
from here. I started my car—blessed air-conditioning—and
backed out far enough to see the Mustang reach the mouth
of the alley. It signaled a left turn, although there was no
other traffic, and pulled out onto the street heading south.

Tailing her was no problem. She drove well under the
speed limit and scrupulously obeyed every traffic law, so
much so you could attribute it to a guilty conscience. We
continued south through residential neighborhoods and cir-

cled the Jewish cemetery, coming out on Harvard. There she signaled a right turn, waited, and made the move. I purposely allowed a couple cars to get between us. The way she was driving, she was creating a mini traffic jam so she would not be able to turn off without my knowing it. Besides, we were headed for the high-level Harvard-Denison Bridge with nowhere to go but straight ahead.

The first major intersection on the far side was West Twenty-fifth Street where the Mustang hugged the left lane and grateful traffic went around her on the right. She turned onto West Twenty-fifth and I followed. This neighborhood south of the zoo, Old Brooklyn, was the part of the city where I had grown up. Old Mr. Waldberg, who had been running his candy store since he had fled the Nazis, was cleaning the windows of his establishment. It was the place where I had stopped to drink Coke and explore the mysteries of life in his extensive collection of magazines and paperbacks. In fact I used to be the one out there cleaning the windows. I wondered if he had never found another boy to do it as well. I honked to him and waved, and he returned the wave, barely looking around. He had no idea it was the crazy Disbro boy who had grown up to be a cop. His predictions would have sent me the other direction, considering some of the escapades I had been involved in. He had thought my only hope of salvation lay in becoming a professional baseball player.

Not that I was headed for a life of crime. My share of hellraising had probably been mild by most measurements, but Mr. Waldberg's Old World standards had a hard time grasping a boy whose ambition inclined him toward baseball and paperback books. Never mind that he made his living selling those books. All his customers were idle dreamers who failed to measure up to his notions of frugal ambition. Maybe he was right. Look how I turned out.

The woman in the green Mustang continued south until ahead I could see the dust rising from the construction around the I-480 freeway. Before we reached the construction site, she made yet another left turn.

The place she entered was an apartment complex, the kind of place that calls itself a village. It covered the equivalent of four city blocks and had its own winding street snaking among a series of low buildings. There was a parking lot in front of each building, always inadequate for the number of cars that needed to park there. Halfway through the complex, she turned into one of the parking areas. I went on to the next unit, whipped around in its parking lot, and came back so I could peer around the corner of the building back to the Mustang. The woman had just got out and was tromping determinedly up the walk toward one of the ground-floor units. The door opened and a man stepped out with a beer can in his hand. He was lanky with a receding chin and a thatch of unruly brown hair. He was an exact replica of a photograph I had seen earlier—Theodore Wyckoff.

When the woman saw Wyckoff, she stopped and said something to him in angry tones. At that distance, even with my window down, I couldn't make out the words, but the melody was plain. He tried something soothing in reply. She hunched her thin shoulders, gripped her biceps and trembled, as if she were having a malarial spasm. Wyckoff said something else. She slapped a set of keys angrily in his palm and stomped into the apartment. Wyckoff shrugged and looked upward, telling God he would never understand women.

Wyckoff finished his beer, crushed the can, and tossed it onto the grass before his apartment. He walked to the back of the Mustang, unlocked the trunk, and picked up the cardboard box. He carried it through the open door of the apartment, returned seconds later, and went again to the Mustang's trunk. This trip he pulled out both suitcases, set one down to free a hand for slamming the lid, and carried the two suitcases into the apartment. The door shut behind him.

Curtain.

There was nothing more for me to see here unless I was ready to brace Wyckoff. Before that happened, I wanted to know what had chased him from his apartment on Fleet. Taking I-77 I made the return trip to Fleet Avenue in a third the time it had taken following the Mustang.

This time I parked in the slot the Mustang had vacated. I went through the gate in the fence and climbed the outside stairs to the third floor and walked down the hall to Wyckoff's apartment. The door was locked, but the fit was not particularly tight. Making sure no one else was in the hall, I got out my wallet and removed the plastic calendar handed out by my insurance company. I slipped the calendar into the crack between the door and the frame at the spring bolt, manipulated a little, and felt the bolt move back enough to allow the door to swing in.

The instant the door opened, I knew what I was going to find. The odor of death, of instant decay, is unmistakable. Violent death, in particular, carries its own variation, death to the max. The shock of impact from the lethal instrument causes the body to tense up. Seconds later, with death's arrival, everything relaxes—feces, urine, everything. Ask any cop about his favorite story of finding a dead body in a closed room in hot weather. Mine is about a man who kicked off from a coronary in August, leaving his five dogs without anyone to feed them. I was tasting the recycled chili dogs I had eaten for lunch as I entered the apartment.

I didn't need my eyes to find him or even my nose. My ears honed in on him like sonar, drawn by the buzz of flies. He had been sitting in a wing-back chair facing the television set, which was not playing now. It occurred to me that the sound could have been turned up high to cover the noise of the shot and then shut off before the neighbors could complain. A reading lamp beside the chair was turned on, which might have been significant of something except that the sun had risen and set several times since he bought the farm. There was no sign of a struggle, but pointing a gun at someone usually minimizes resistance.

I looked away from the peripherals to the dead man. Forty-odd, stout, dressed in a Hawaiian shirt and gray slacks. He had worn a full beard, dark with streaks of gray, and a full head of the same hair long enough to cover his ears and his collar. There was a bald spot on top the size of a coaster. His head lolled back, a thick tongue filling his slack mouth, arms hanging down over the chair arms, legs out with the heels of his Tony Lama cowboy boots pushing grooves through the nap of the carpet. The only wound I could see was a bullet hole below his left eye. The slug had gouged a groove along the left side of his nose as it entered. The skin looked scorched, meaning very close range. The size of the entrance wound was consistent with a .38 Special, about as far as I would go with guessing. The exit wound in the back of his head was much larger. A soggy mass of blood, brain tissue, and bone fragments had sprayed across the headrest of the chair like a macabre antimacassar. It had had time to dry and stiffen.

"Don't go away," I said to him and turned my attention to the rest of the apartment. In the bedroom the closet and the dresser drawers were empty. In the bathroom the shelves of the medicine cabinet were bare. In the kitchen the refrigerator had only a few items that could have been abandoned with no loss. There were dishes on the shelves and silverware in the drawers, but they looked like the kind of mismatched pieces that would go with a furnished apartment. It seemed the woman had managed to cram all of Wyckoff's personal items into two suitcases and a cardboard box.

My foot crunched something on the floor, broken glass, the remains of a drinking glass. I remembered the sound of the crash and a gasp when I had knocked on the door. I now knew the woman had been in here alone with the corpse, packing Wyckoff's things. I gave her credit for sticking it out longer than I could.

The telephone was in the living room on an end table under a knick-knack shelf. I had the receiver in my hand, reaching for the ancient rotary dial, when I noticed something on the shelf at my eye level. A black leather spring-clip holster. I took it down, seeing the inside leather was worn from much fast-draw practice. On the back the size of the gun that would fit into it had been stamped into the leather: "Colt 2", Det. Spec., Cobra, Agent." I put it back where I had found it and dialed 555-5464, which happens to be the number of the Cleveland Homicide Unit.

6

MANNY AGOSTA STAYED in the apartment the bare minimum of time required of a Homicide detective at the scene of the crime before he came out to join me on the rear balcony. "Jesus!" he said and took a deep breath that found the humid air refreshing.

I was sitting on the balcony rail, my back against the side of the building, smoking and waiting for my interrogation. The uniforms who had responded in the zone car had taken one look at the situation and realized there was little likelihood the murderer would still be on the scene and I was probably not him. Their questioning had been cursory and then they set up a guard to secure the scene for Homicide, as the manual dictates.

Now Agosta stood looking out across the rooftops. He was wearing a white short-sleeve shirt and tie but had left his suit jacket in his car, meaning the hardware on his belt was exposed. He wore his sidearm on his right side in one of those holsters split down the front so the gun doesn't have to be drawn, merely pushed forward. He also wore bullet dumps on his left side and handcuffs at his back.

"How's it going, Gil?" he asked, still looking over the rooftops.

"All right until the dead body fell into my lap."

"Still bounty hunting for Glickman?"

"About half the time. The other half I'm working on my own investigations."

"Like what you're doing?"

"It beats hell out of patrolling a shopping mall."

"Which was it brought you here?" Agosta's accent, I realized, was nearly gone. About all that remained was an odd Ricardo Montalban inflection on an occasional word. "Glickman's case or your own?"

"My own."

He faced me, letting me see his Aztec features headon. His eyes dared me to lie. "Want to tell me about it?"

"Missing persons, and not much of a case at that. I came here looking for Wyckoff only because he had been looking for the same guy last week. I wanted to touch base with him to see if he had learned anything."

Agosta waited, as if he expected me to add something. "No names?"

"Not relevant at this time."

"Shitfuck. You're not going to play that game with me, are you?"

"Tell you what, Manny. Give me the name of the snitch who helped you solve your last big case and I'll fill you in."

Agosta nearly allowed a smile to inhabit his lips. He walked over to the balcony rail and sat on it facing me, his arms braced tight at his sides. "How did you come to find the body?"

I took a final drag on my cigarette and flicked it away. "I knocked on his door. I got no answer. I knocked again a little harder and the door swung in. It seems the last person to shut the door didn't give it a shove hard enough to snap the lock in place. I pushed it open. And then I smelled him. Then I looked inside and called you."

"That bullshit is exactly what I hear every day to justify illegal entries. Do you carry a shim?"

"How can I answer a question like that? No man with a credit card in his wallet could clear that one."

"Let it go." Agosta wiped a hand over his jaw. "You got any ideas on this one?"

"Me? I don't work for Homicide."

"You're ahead of me on this one," Agosta admitted. "You know things I don't."

"Not much. I only started on the case a few hours ago."

Agosta waited. I fished a cigarette out of my pocket and lit it, watching the exhaled smoke hang in the still air. "The stiff isn't the guy who rents the apartment."

"Sure of that?"

"Unless all my information on Wyckoff's description is wrong by a mile. The dead man is twice as old, half as tall, and three times as wide. The one picture I saw of Wyckoff showed him clean shaven."

"Goddamn!" Agosta considered the information. "Why do you have to complicate my life? If the stiff isn't Wyckoff, who is he?"

"I've got an idea on that. It's just a wild-ass guess."

"I'll listen."

"John Monk."

"No shit? The baby snatcher?"

"Uh-huh."

Agosta stood up, paced to the far end of the balcony, and came back to me. "You searched the body? Found his ID?"

"I told you it was only a wild-ass guess. He matches the Monk's description and I have some reason to believe the Monk might have been called into the missing-persons case. You should be able to verify it easy enough."

"Fuck! Why do you have to tell me these things?"

"You asked me."

Agosta slapped a pillar supporting the roof over the balcony, probably because he couldn't reach me. "You have to come along and complicate things. Christ! Wanta know something? Until you dumped this shit on me, I was ready to write this one off. You believe that?"

"If you say so. Hell, do you think I'm going to contradict you?"

Agosta sat on the railing again and this time braced his arms on his knees. "Consider this: If it wasn't for the damned gun missing, I'd be half-convinced the case was a suicide."

"For sure?"

"I said 'half-convinced.' You saw the wound, right? You saw the way the muzzle flash burned the flesh? The groove the bullet gouged along the side of his nose? How do you read that?"

"The killer stood with the muzzle only inches away from his face. He was aiming for dead center, right between the eyes, and jerked off slightly when he pulled the trigger."

"Now take the same facts and look at it like this." Agosta pointed his forefinger and turned it to his own face. "There he is looking down the gun barrel, probably operating the trigger with his thumb. That pulls the aim off dead center but close enough to get the job done. It works out that way except for the gun. It should have fallen in his lap or on the floor beside his chair, even been clutched in his hand. But it's gone, so it looks like it has to be murder. What I'm wondering is, did someone take the gun away so we'd rule out suicide?"

That was my cue. I let it pass, feeling my conscience plucking a string.

Agosta gave up being subtle. "Tell me you didn't do that."

"I didn't," I said truthfully. "I left everything the way I found it. That's Rule One."

"I had to ask."

"Christ, Manny, that body has been in there what? Five days? A week? The door wasn't shut tight so anyone could have wandered in and out in that time. Even if the door had been locked, the guy who lives there, Wyckoff, must have a key. He could have returned twice a day in that time. Or he could have given the key to someone else, who could have had a duplicate made to pass around. God knows what traffic has been through there."

"I'll stick with keeping it simple. Where would I find Wyckoff?"

"This is where he lives and he's not here. Other than that, all I know about him is that he attends Cleveland State."

"Then I'll have to go there."

"Suppose you're right on this one, Manny. Suppose someone did cart the gun away. What would that accomplish?"

Agosta had to think that one over. "Maybe the guy has a clause in his insurance policy that won't pay off for suicide. For whatever reason, he wants to kill himself and still have his family provided for, so he sets things up with somebody—Wyckoff—to make his death look like murder."

I smiled and flipped my cigarette away. "I always said watching too much television softens your mind."

"Say what you want, I'm onto something. Now let's talk about the Monk, if that's who it is. What brings him to Cleveland?"

"My missing-persons case has an eight-year-old kid involved. At one point the grandparents were threatening to call in the Monk because they think the father, a widower, is unfit. Father and son have both taken off—maybe."

"Why maybe?"

"The father's on vacation and the kid's out of school. There's no reason they would have to check with anybody for the next couple months."

"What kind of job does the father have that allows that much time off?"

"College professor."

"Teaching where?"

"Cleveland State."

"Where Wyckoff goes."

"Along with twenty thousand others."

Agosta shook his head in disgust. "I don't like this, Gil. Everything you tell me keeps turning back on itself. I really wanta cut your slack but I'm gonna need a name. Who's the professor?"

I considered. There was no reason from my client's standpoint to withhold Gault's name. Monica would probably have welcomed the aid of the police department searching for him. In fact, she had once tried to go to them. Getting Gault's name into the computer system would be a big help if he happened to get a parking ticket in Boise. So I laid it all on Agosta, everything I had learned so far today—except for what I had seen of the woman in the Mustang. It was a lead I could follow on my own to stay ahead of the police.

"And that's all you knew about Wyckoff when you came here?" Agosta asked.

"I was hoping to learn some more but the stiff wouldn't talk."

"Figure the dead man is the Monk. Figure he was hooked up with Wyckoff. Figure they snatched Gault's kid and brought him here. Gault comes after the kid and kills the Monk getting him free. Now Gault and the kid are on the run together, maybe being chased by Wyckoff."

"What happened to the suicide theory?" I asked.

"I'm trying not to overlook anything."

"The trouble with fitting Gault to the crime is that you don't have one bit of evidence."

"Evidence," Agosta explained, "is what you find after you know what you're looking for."

"Other people might call that building a frame."

"Let 'em. From you I'm going to need a written statement."

That took half an hour. Agosta provided the paper and a clipboard and I used my own pen. While I was doing it, the coroner's van arrived and carted away the remains. Finished with the statement, I showed it to Agosta, who read it like a teacher grading a student's theme. In the end, I passed except for one point.

"Your handwriting needs improvement," Agosta told me. He was not the first to observe that.

"How can I ever be charged with making false statements if no one can decipher what it says?"

Agosta folded the statement and stuck it in his hip pocket. He had come back from the apartment holding a manila property envelope which, experience told me, probably held the contents of the dead man's pockets. He dug into it and handed me a couple laminated cards. One was an Indiana driver's license, the other a private investigator's license, also from Indiana. Both held photos of the dead man and gave his name as John H. Monk.

"Every broken clock is right twice a day," Agosta observed. "Looks like you hit it on this one."

I returned the documents. "Anything else you need from me?"

"Not for the moment. Be available if the spirit moves me to come looking for you."

My watch showed 4:05, time for me to chase after Wyckoff in his apartment on Broadview. I left Agosta on the balcony and started down the stairs. I got only as far as the first landing when Agosta said, "One more thing."

I stopped and looked up at him leaning over the balcony rail.

"We had a deal. If you opened up to me, I was supposed to give you the man who helped me clear my last big case." Agosta smiled then. "His name was Gil Disbro."

7

THE GREEN MUSTANG was gone from its parking space in the apartment village when I got there ten minutes later. I parked in the space it had occupied and walked up to the apartment door Wyckoff and the woman had entered. There was a picture window into its living room, but it was covered by a heavy drape that told me nothing of what was inside. I rang the bell in the middle of the door and stepped aside, out of range of the peephole that was part of the bell assembly.

The door opened and the woman looked out. It was the first time I had seen her up close after keeping her under observation most of the afternoon. Distance had flattered her. At this range her face was no match for her body. It was too elongated and her cheeks were pitted with mementos of teenage acne. Her eyes tried to focus on a point over my left shoulder. They were a shade that would vary at different times, showing green for the moment.

"Where's Ted?" I asked.

"Ted?" She had to think about it. "Gone."

I pushed the door open and stepped past her into the apartment. "Sure he's not inside?"

She watched me walk past her, blinked, and said slowly, "Hey."

"Hey yourself. I'm Gil. Ted probably told you about me." She tried to recall. "No-o-o."

By that time I was inside shutting the door behind me. "It's all right. Ted told me everything."

"About what?" She wanted to be indignant but doubt held her in check.

I looked around suspiciously. "Sure there's no one here?" When her bobbing head had assured me, I said, "The apartment on Fleet. The man sitting in the chair."

"God!" Suddenly her legs went out on a job action. She wobbled to the nearest piece of furniture, a couch, and sat on it heavily. "Too much."

The furniture in the place was all from discount stores where you provided the U-haul trailer to transport it home. It was cheap vinyl and pressed wood. Any money spent in the place had gone into the TV-stereo-VCR setup stacked on shelves, and into the coke mirror on the coffee table, with a line of white powder laid out on it, which went a long way toward explaining her slow-motion synapses. While I watched, she picked up a short length of glass tube and snorted a toot. She fell back and laid her head on the couch while she waited for the rush.

"What's your name?" I asked.

"Bobbie." She sighed and smiled at whatever visions the nose candy gave her. "Actually it's Roberta."

"Sure, that explains it. I've heard Ted mention you, but I thought it was a guy."

"Happens all the time."

I had been roaming about, peeking here and there, and now my travels brought me to the kitchen. It was a tiny place with barely enough room to walk between the counter and the appliances. Bobbie's purse, the same one she had been carrying earlier, was sitting on the counter. I managed to glom it without actually entering the kitchen. I carried it back to the living room and sat on a footstool to look into it.

"What do you think you're doing?" Bobbie asked.

"Getting the gun. Ted thought it would be better if I had it." I sorted through the contents I had seen spill out in the parking lot and found the only item that interested me. It was a Colt Cobra, the same model as the Detective Special except this one was made with aluminum parts to keep its weight to a minimum. I dropped the cylinder out and examined the chambers. Five live rounds and one dented primer, which had been under the hammer. I punched the bullets partway out of the chambers and plucked one out for examination. They were home-made loads with flat-nosed wadcutter heads seated reversed, a mean slug that could have done the number on the Monk, if it had the kind of souped-up powder load I suspected. With the cylinder still hanging out, I looked down the muzzle while using my thumbnail for a reflector. The unjacketed wadcutter slug had left lead deposits and powder residue in the rifling grooves. I closed the cylinder and dropped the Colt into my side jacket pocket.

"Where did Ted go?"

Bobbie shrugged. "Out on some business."

"When will he be back?"

"When he's finished."

I dug a little farther in her purse until I found her wallet and looked at her Ohio driver's license, issued only this April. Roberta W. Slack, twenty-three, this address.

"What do you think you're doing?" she complained listlessly. "That's my purse."

"That's what I thought. If it belonged to someone else, I wouldn't bother with it." The money compartment of her billfold held seventeen dollars and a bunch of payroll stubs from Wally's Tavern on Snow Road in Parma.

"You've got a lot of nerve." She sprang off the couch and snatched her purse back. "If a person didn't know better, I'd think you was a cop."

"That's rich. Was I a cop, knowing what I know, you'd be on your way to a cell in Marysville."

"Jesus! Ain't that the truth." Having rescued her purse, she tossed it carelessly to one end of the couch and sat down again, this time setting her elbows on her knees and running her fingers through her hair. She stared down at her own reflection in the coke mirror and then looked up at me. "You wouldn't be Ted's connection?"

"Why?"

"I was wondering, could you get me another toot?"

"Haven't you had enough?"

"There's no such thing when your mind is full of the pictures mine is."

"The dead man?"

Her head bobbed like one of those dogs in the rear window of a car. "God, it was gross! The guy had been dead nearly a week. I never thought it would be like that."

I lit a cigarette and got up to hand it to Bobbie, who took it and drew on it gratefully. "Why did you let Ted send you there?"

"Why do I ever do what he wants? He cons me into it. Besides, he promised me a couple lids."

I lit another cigarette, for myself this time. "You should have told him to go himself."

"Don't I know it? He claimed he didn't want to be seen around his apartment."

"Why not? It's his place."

"God, you sound like Ted. Tell it again—again—again."

"I sound like Ted because I'm working his side of the street. Help me and you're helping him."

"After what Ted put me through, I got no reason to help him."

"Sure. Desert him now. See if my connection ever gets here." I stood up, halfheartedly turning toward the exit.

"You've got a connection?"

"Best you'll ever snort."

Bobbie pointed to the footstool. "Don't go away. I'll answer your questions."

I sat again.

"Here's the truth. Last week Ted comes over here, says he wants to crash with me a couple days on account of his apartment being used for something else. What, he wouldn't say, but you know how Ted is always talking. He's always going to make the big deal, always going to hit the jackpot, only it'll be tomorrow or the day after. Somehow he never catches up to that day. Hell, I've been listening to that kind of talk ever since high school days in Decatur. This time he claimed he had the lowdown on some dude who would pay to hush it up. I quit listening. I quit listening to him years ago."

Bobbie was speaking in a flat voice, running through the facts by rote. She inhaled another drag off her cigarette and resumed: "So I let him crash here a few days. That was

Tuesday. Wednesday he borrowed my Mustang and went to class. You know he enrolled in college? Wednesday evening I was home on account of that's my day off. Sunday and Wednesday. Thursday he stayed around my place, saying he was waiting for a phone call. Maybe and maybe not. Anyway, when it was time for me to go to work, he drove me so he could use my Mustang to check on his apartment. I went to work in the bar and didn't see him until almost closing time. He didn't look right when he came in and he started gulping down beers as fast as I could pour them. I knew something was wrong, but I figured another deal had gone sour. He got good and bombed that night, but the next day he was up early getting a newspaper. That's Ted Wyckoff I'm talking about, who never read a whole newspaper in his life. Suddenly he's reading every goddamned page, studying it.

"But that isn't all. He starts listening to the news on the radio. In here or out in the car, he's got to hear the news every time it comes on. That still isn't all. Know what he did next? He used my VCR to tape the news shows. You believe that? News shows? I mean, he had a regular schedule. At five o'clock he watched Channel 5. At six o'clock, he watched Channel 3 and taped Channel 8. At six-thirty, he watched the second half hour of Channel 8, and then at seven, he switched back to Channel 3 for their second go-round. After that he played back the tape. What do you make of that?"

"There was one particular story he was looking for."

"Bet your ass there was. Only he never told me about it. So this goes on all weekend and into Monday. Finally I ask what he wants. He says a little favor. He wants me to stop at his apartment and pick up his things. That sounds simple enough, so I say all right. Then he lays the rest of it on me. Oh, yeah, don't get excited if you happen to see a dead body there. I go spastic. No way am I going into a room with a dead body. But Ted starts turning on the charm. At last I agree. I'll do it on my day off, on Wednesday, today."

She crushed out her cigarette and popped up onto her feet, then began pacing around the living room. A few minutes ago she had been listless, on the verge of falling asleep. Now she was so hyper she couldn't sit still. Shows you what nose candy will do.

"I used Ted's key to get into the apartment," she resumed. "I did my best to ignore the dead body. I went straight to the bedroom and packed most of Ted's things in two suitcases. There was still more left over that I put in an old cardboard box. I carried the suitcases down and put them in the trunk of my car. I went back up to the apartment to get the box— and do the rest."

"Which was?" I prompted.

"For one thing, to get the gun. Ted said I would find it on the floor by the chair. He wanted me to pick it up and bring it back with me. I didn't like that. I asked would it go off and Ted said don't worry, it wouldn't as long as I didn't touch the trigger. He said pick it up by the handle and drop it in my purse and it would be all right."

"Where did you find it, exactly." I got off the footstool and indicated the nearest chair. "Show me."

"About here." Her toe indicated a point on her carpet about two feet from the right leg, angling away from the chair. I visualized a man sitting in that chair who had just shot himself in the face. I made allowances for the recoil of the light revolver and the reflexive jerk of the suicide's arm as it flopped down onto the arm of the chair. The revolver could easily have landed on Bobbie's toe.

"What did Ted want with the gun?"

"Beats hell out of me. He didn't even want it when I got

back. He asked did I get it and I said yeah, it's in my purse. He didn't even look at it. Jesus! If I'd known that was all he wanted, I wouldn't of had to bring it back. I could have dropped it in a garbage can." She corrugated her brow in thought. "Are you sure I should be telling you all this?"

"Chrissake! Haven't I done enough already to prove you can trust me?" I complained petulantly.

She thought about that and apparently recalled some proof of good faith I didn't know about. "I guess so. Ted was right about one thing. The gun wouldn't go off by accident. I dropped it, you know, when I was coming out of the building. I had my purse on top of the box I was carrying. When I was coming out of the gate in back, I was juggling the box and my purse fell off and the gun spilled out. That was a fright."

"I'll bet."

"But the gun wasn't the worst part, like I thought it would be. The worst part was getting the key."

"The key?" I tried to sound knowledgeable at the same time I was asking a question.

"To the motel room. That's what else Ted wanted and it was in the dead guy's pocket. I had to go through his clothes to find it. Gross! He had crapped himself and pissed his pants. Would you have thought a dead man would do that?"

"What was the name of the motel?"

"It was on Brookpark Road out toward the airport. Dream-something. The room number was 14."

"Why did Ted want the key?"

"Something to do with the big deal. He doesn't tell me everything. Don't you know what this is all about?"

"Some of it." I had been pushing my luck with her, getting more information than I had a right to because she was wired.

I looked at my watch. "How soon is Ted due back?"

"Who knows? He claimed he was going to that motel I told you about." A smile worked itself into the corners of her mouth. "Maybe we could think of ways to kill some time. You wouldn't be hard to take, and God knows I could use a little relaxation."

Worse offers have been tossed at me but not many with less appeal. "I'd hate to upset Ted."

She puzzled over that. "What business is it of his?"

"Well, he's been staying here. I thought he was more than your star boarder."

"You think we've been screwing?" The idea really upset her for a few seconds until something occurred to her to give it a humorous spin. She laughed. "I get it. You're going by my name, Slack. That was my married name, but I've been divorced a couple years now. My name is Roberta W. Slack. W for *Wyckoff*. I'm Ted's sister."

8

LEAVING BOBBIE'S APARTMENT, I turned south on Broadview, crossed the freeway construction, and turned west on
Brookpark Road, aiming for Cleveland Hopkins Airport
seven miles down the road. Both sides of the road were
generously stocked with pizza joints, used-car lots, fast-food
franchises, gas stations, car washes, drive-in banks, drive-in
theaters, discount stores, and even some motels. I was
watching for one with the word *Dream* in its name.

The death of John Monk in Wyckoff's apartment raised so
many possibilities I was fighting to keep my mind from
running amok with them all. Monk had come all the way
from Indiana to look up Wyckoff, but with what purpose in
mind? What would Wyckoff gain by making Monk's suicide

look like a murder? Or had someone been there before to pass a murder off as a suicide? Suppositions were stacking up on speculations. I shook them all off.

I had escaped Bobbie's apartment without succumbing to her invitation. I wanted to catch Wyckoff at the motel to find out what his scam was and maybe learn why he was trying to make a suicide look like a murder.

DREAMLAND MOTEL
$25 (SINGLE) UP

It was on the Cleveland side of the road, an L-shaped structure that could have been planted along any highway anywhere in the country. I turned into its parking lot and drove directly to the door with the metal numerals 14 screwed into it. No green Mustang anywhere but a midnight blue Lincoln Continental with Indiana plates occupied the slot out front.

I parked next to the Lincoln and walked up to the door. I listened first, tested the knob enough to learn it was locked, and tried knocking as a last resort. All that accomplished was wear and tear on the door. I turned away from the room and tried the car. It, too, was locked. The car looked as if the owner took pride in it, but a thin film of road dust had collected on it, polka-dotted with clean spots where raindrops might have hit. Our last trace of precipitation, as the TV weathermen reported, had been three days ago. Birds had been dive-bombing the Lincoln, leaving white and purple samples on hood, windshield, roof, and trunk. Inside, the plush interior was bare except for a Hardee's bag stuffed into the wastebasket on the transmission hump. It was equipped with a CB radio, a Fuzzbuster, and a cellular telephone.

So much for the car. I left mine where it was and walked to

the center of the motel where it made its right-angle turn, and pushed through a door marked *Office*. Two steps across the threshold was a counter, and behind the counter a curtained arch into living quarters. A bell had jingled when I opened the door, causing sounds of movement in the living quarters. The curtain parted and a man stepped through snarling, "Yeah?" in a tone that implied he was not finding a great deal of fulfillment with his career in motel management.

"I'm interested in Unit 14."

He looked at a chart on a clipboard under the counter. "It's rented." He was forty-something, old enough to have a few gray hairs mixed in his beard stubble and on his chest and protruding marsupial pouch. I could see that because his shirt was unbuttoned. Besides the shirt, he wore a pair of wild Hawaiian shorts that were mostly red, and a pair of thongs that clopped like hoofs when he walked.

"Being occupied is what makes it interesting." I showed him my ID card.

"No way. The owner's got a policy against getting involved in divorce cases." The clerk had sharp, gaunt features that suggested there were circumstances under which he could be persuaded to forget policy.

"This isn't a divorce matter." I put away my photo and showed him a picture of a prominent Federalist—Alexander Hamilton engraved on a twenty-dollar bill. Keeping a tight grip on my money, I added, "I would like to have a look at the registration card and hear anything you can tell me."

The clerk divided his attention between Hamilton and me, finding it easier to look Hamilton square in the eye. "I shouldn't."

"Who's to know?"

He brought out a small metal file box big enough for five-by-seven cards, and flipped through it to the one he wanted. It had been dated last Monday and the signature was a scrawl that could have said "J. Miller" as well as anything, of Indianapolis. The box for the car listed a Lincoln and an Indiana plate that matched the one outside.

"He's been here awhile," I noted.

The clerk eyed the twenty. "When he first checked in, he paid for a couple days in advance. Said he wasn't sure how long his business would take. When that was up, he paid for a week in advance. Let's see, that will expire at check-out time tomorrow."

"What did he look like?"

"Not very tall but powerful build, like a weight lifter. Forty, long dark hair and a beard. Dressed in casual clothes."

"Has he been coming and going regularly?"

"The last time I saw him was a week ago when he paid for his room. That doesn't mean he hasn't been here." The clerk propped his skinny arms on the counter. "Maybe you'd like to know what the maid told me."

"Maybe I would."

His eyes drifted down to the twenty. I loosened my grip and it leaped into his pocket. "The maid tells me his bed hasn't been slept in and it doesn't look like he's even been in the room. Ash trays are empty, the wastebasket doesn't have anything in it, and the blister seals over the glasses haven't been broken."

None of which surprised me. "Has anybody been here looking for him?"

"Not that I've seen."

"His car is still sitting in his parking space. Looks like it's been there the whole time."

"So I noticed."

"Then how did he leave?"

"I can't say." But he was not devoid of ideas. He leaned across the counter, breathing a beery odor on me. "Last time I saw him was a week ago, when he paid for his room. It was about this time of day. He asked me where he could get a meal and I steered him to the restaurant two doors down, the Chinese place. He asked was it worth driving there and I said not to bother, you can cut right across the Stop'N'Go and you're there. Suppose he did that, and while he was in the restaurant he called a taxi or a friend, or maybe he was picked up by a rich dame with a chauffeur driving her Mercedes, who took him out to her mansion in Pepper Pike."

"You're sure no one was here earlier today looking for him?"

"No one stopped here in the office. Had they went directly to his room, I wouldn't know about it."

Or entered with a key taken from the customer's dead body. I held out my hand. "I'll need your key."

"What for?"

"So I can get into his room without damaging his door." I kept my palm out.

"I can't do that."

"Then come along and unlock the door for me."

The strain of greed got the best of him. "A deposit. I need a deposit on the key."

Arguing with him would only have delayed matters. I found a five-dollar bill in my loose change pocket and shoved it his way. He traded me the passkey for the five with no more pain than having a molar extracted. The key was attached to a paddle with the name of the Dreamland Motel but no room number, only a *P*. Dropping it in my pocket, I left the office and strolled down to 14 again.

No one was watching me. I slipped the key into the lock, turned it, and slid through the crack, shutting the door after me. I pulled the curtains shut over the only window before I turned on the lights and looked at the place where I found myself. Standard motel room. Table with two chairs in front of the window. Bed with a dresser at the foot. Closet a niche in the wall with no door over it. Sink and mirror at back. Bathroom beside the sink. I advanced stealthily, missing the feel of a piece in my hand. It would have been a good time to pull out the Colt Cobra I had taken from Bobbie, but that was locked away in the trunk of my car. I looked into the bathroom, the only place anyone could have been hiding, and found no one. Toilet and bathtub with shower curtain open. A blue terrycloth robe hung on a peg on the back of the door.

I turned away from the bathroom to see what spoor Monk had left here. His travel kit sat on the side of the sink, unzipped and open as if he were displaying his toilet articles—comb, toothbrush, deodorant, hairspray, no razor. The rest of his luggage was in the closet niche, a soft leather suitcase with zipper pouches on the outside and a suitbag hanging from the rod. The bag held two summer-weight suits and two neckties draped around the suit hanger, neither of which quite matched either suit. A pair of Hush Puppies were in the bottom of the suitbag and a pair of wingtips in the pocket behind the suits. I investigated the suitcase without dumping its contents. Boxer shorts, socks, two white shirts with short sleeves, and one sport shirt that might have supported a solid tie in a pinch. Back in a corner of the closet was a laundry bag like a gunny sack with a drawstring top. I dumped that out on the floor. Five pair of socks, five pair of boxer shorts, two sport shirts, one white shirt, two handkerchiefs. I put everything back in the laundry bag ready for my big deduction: Monk had been on the road five days.

One more piece of luggage, an attaché case, open on the bed, its contents spilled out, papers scattered across the cover, some on the floor. I gathered them up and carried them over to the table to inspect them. Most were blank forms Monk had had printed up for use in his detective business. I recognized them because the ones I use are similar. A cover sheet to start any case—name of client, address, other pertinent data, a space for an explanation of the case. A follow-up page with headings to identify the case and then twenty-five blank lines to record a narrative of the investigation. A statement form with the Miranda warning printed on it. A suspect-description form with all kinds of data on clothes, physical details, and habits to be checked off—used mainly to jog the memory of witnesses. A log for recording mileage and use of the company car, mandatory these days courtesy of the IRS. An expense account form. The top pages of the pads of these last two forms had been at least partly filled out.

I lit a cigarette while I studied the information. The automobile log showed he had left Indianapolis on Friday, July 11, and driven to Cincinnati. The expense account (charge to: Wesley Hammond) showed he had checked into the Netherlands Hilton ($54), although the receipt with it showed the Quality Inn ($27). He had stayed in Cincinnati Saturday and Sunday, July 12–13, adding sixty-two miles to his odometer listed as "Cincinnati and environs." On Monday, July 14, he drove to Cleveland and, for expense account purposes, checked into the Bond Court Hotel. He had not filled in the expenses for the rest of his life.

So I could show that Monk had padded his expense account. Had he been so guilt-ridden about that he had killed himself? More significant was the fact he had been hired by Wesley Hammond. That piece of news suggested even more ideas.

I carried his papers back to the attaché case and threw them in. Being thorough, I also checked the lid of the case where there were some pockets. In one of the pockets was a pair of maps, standard AAA issue that showed Cincinnati and Cleveland. Being a stranger from another state, he would naturally want maps of the two Ohio cities he intended to visit. Still worth looking at. I unfolded the Cleveland map first because that was the one I knew best. Even the AAA divided the city east and west, one on either side of the paper. It unfolded so that I saw the east side first. There were marks on the map that hadn't been there when it was printed, bold circles drawn with a red felt-tip pen. One in Cleveland Heights that included Gault's house. One around the campus of Cleveland State. One in Slavic Village on Fleet—Wyckoff's apartment. One around Bobbie's place off Broadview. I had the eerie feeling someone had been recording the places I had visited that day.

I spread the map out on the bed to look at the west side. A circle for the Dreamland Motel. A circle for Arlene's apartment in Lakewood. One more circle I couldn't account for where Denison, Clark, Lorain, and West Boulevard come together with the I-90 freeway. I tried to visualize what would be there. All I could see was a few blocks of nondescript buildings, maybe houses on the side streets, maybe flats above the stores. I folded the Cleveland map and tried the one for Cincinnati. There were more red marks on this one that meant very little to me. A couple were on the north side around the University of Cincinnati. One surrounded police headquarters in front of what used to be Union Station. One in Indian Hill. One across the river in Newport, Kentucky, which barely made it onto the bottom of the map. Others I didn't know. Driving from one to another could easily have added up to sixty-two miles.

When I left, I took both maps with me, as well as the

automobile log and the expense account. The desk clerk was busy checking in a family with West Virginia plates on the station wagon outside, so I tossed the passkey onto the counter and walked back outside to check one last detail. A narrow strip of grass separated the motel parking lot from the Stop'N'Go lot next door. Footsteps had worn a bare path through the grass between the two lots. I took it, crossed the Stop'N'Go lot and came to the Chinese restaurant in less than a minute. A door led into a vestibule from which another door led into the restaurant proper. Pay phones were in the vestibule. I dropped a quarter in one and punched out Helen's home phone, figuring that if she hadn't got back from class, I could at least leave a message on her answering machine. As it turned out, her voice was live.

I said, "Hi, sweetheart. I'm still working. If you haven't popped anything in the microwave, how would you like to meet me for dinner?"

"Who is this?"

"Sorry, you just missed your last chance for a free meal."

"Let me reconsider. Robert Redford has other commitments this week, so you must be Gil Disbro."

"Robert Redford? For God's sake, I'm not only better looking than he is, I'm taller."

"You're taller," she agreed.

"Couldn't you at least have guessed Philip Marlowe? Lew Archer? Sam Spade?"

"Amos Walker?"

"I'm buying dinner—on Monica Brodbeck's expense account."

"Where?"

"It has to be in the vicinity of Lorain and West Boulevard. Got any ideas?"

"I can't think of anything near there except a Burger Chef."

"Then that's where we'll meet. I'm out near Hopkins airport, so it's going to take me awhile to get there. Wait for me in the parking lot."

I hung up before she could ask for any explanations and strolled back to my car.

9

HELEN'S HOUSE, the place where we cohabit, is on Bridge Avenue in Cleveland, in the part of town that was once a separate community on the west bank of the Cuyahoga River known as Ohio City. This late in the twentieth century, the neighborhood is being gentrified by the Yuppie crowd. From Ohio City to the mystery circle on Monk's map was only a little over two miles down Lorain Avenue. Of course, this time of day she had to fight rush-hour traffic.

My route was much longer, but at least I was not entangled with traffic. Not surprisingly, Helen's black and gray Honda Accord was already in the parking lot of the Burger Chef when I arrived. I pulled up behind her and she got out wearing the same outfit I'd seen her in at noon, now carrying a milk shake in her hand as she approached the passenger side of my Caprice.

"Twenty years have just dropped off my shoulders," she commented as she swung into my seat. She closed her door and sipped her milk shake through the straw. "I haven't done this since I was a teenager."

"Calories."

"Spoilsport."

I joined the line of cars entering the drive-through and ordered a large black coffee through the microphone. The machine didn't seem to believe me because a disembodied voice asked, "Will that be small or large?"

"Large."

"Cream?"

"No."

"Sugar?"

"No."

"Anything else?"

"No."

"Please pick up your order at the window."

I pulled up to the window, paid for it, and received it in a sack from an adolescent girl trying to look like Molly Ringwald. "Cream or sugar?" she asked with a smile.

"No." When such a complex order had at last been filled, I pulled on through the line and entered a parking space as close to Lorain Avenue as I could get. Helen slid across the seat until her thigh touched mine. I sipped my coffee and studied the cityscape before me, marveling at the tendency of every busy street in America to look like Los Angeles. Helen slurped to the bottom of her milkshake while her left hand played lightly along my inner thigh. I could have gone on like that for a long time.

"Why are we doing this?" Helen asked at last.

"I'm detecting." I got out the map of Cleveland I had stolen from Monk's room and showed her the mystery circle in which we sat. I explained to her a little of how I had acquired it. "Something in this area, probably within our sight, has a significance. I'm trying to imagine what it could be."

She studied the map and then the scene before us. "Let's try eliminating some places. It's not the paperback exchange, not the Laundromat, not the video store, not—"

"All those places have flats upstairs," I pointed out. "Someone could be living there."

"We can come back to that." She went on down the block naming places as unlikely. When she reached the end, she slipped on her glasses and started the next block. "What does that sign say, the one with the arrow pointing down the alley?"

" 'Ernie's Body Shop.' " *Bing!* I reached into the backseat of my car over Helen's shoulders and dug the copy of Wyckoff's transcript out of my file boxes. I ran my eyes down the information to the question I wanted. Employer: Ernie's Body Shop, with an address in the 9500 block of Lorain. "Let's give it a try."

I tossed our empty cardboard cups into the trash can as I pulled out onto the street and headed for the body shop. The alley ran only a short distance from Lorain until it dead-ended at the brink of the freeway ravine. The body shop was a low brick garage at the very end. Leaving Helen in the car, I walked up to the door, which supported a sign telling me the place closed at four o'clock. I tried the door anyway and learned the sign had spoken the truth.

Smack! It was the sound of a butcher slapping a steak on the counter and it had come from around the corner of the building. I headed that way to see what was causing it. There was a chain-link fence back there surrounding the wrecks brought here to await the body shop's attention. Outside the fence was a small parking area holding only two cars at the moment—a green Mustang and a blue Fiat. Two men were in the parking lot duking it out. I leaned against the wall and watched the progress of the fight.

A generation brought up on John Wayne movies has a misconception of what a good fistfight looks like. Hollywood always stages them with the camera in mind and enough careful choreography for a ballet. Real life is different. The combatants either grab each other and roll around on the ground or they stay on their feet and flail away, connecting with one punch in ten. These two were on their feet, socking lots of particulate matter and grunting to show how much effort they were putting into it. The one facing my direction was Wyckoff. As I watched they circled so that Wyckoff's back was to me and I got a look at his opponent. Alan Gault.

I lit a cigarette.

"Shouldn't you do something about it?" Helen had come up beside me to watch around my shoulder.

"Let them go. They'll wear themselves out and we'll deal with the winner."

"They could get hurt."

"Not the way they're going about it."

Helen stood it for only a few seconds more. "Gil, please stop them."

Not the first man in world history to be egged into doing the wrong thing by a woman, I flipped away my half-smoked cigarette and stepped forward, sensible enough to stay out of their range. "Break it up."

Wyckoff turned his head in my direction. The fighting Ph.D. threw everything he had into a sucker punch to Wyckoff's exposed jaw. Wyckoff's head snapped back and he went down—still conscious but stunned. Gault wasted no time gloating over his victory. He scooped up something from the ground I had not noticed before—a manila file folder. The papers it contained should have been scattered by the wind, but in this case they were held in place by a metal clasp at the top. With the papers in hand, Gault dashed for the Fiat.

"Professor! Wait!"

It didn't work. Gault threw the papers into the car, dived across the front seat, and reached for the glove box. I started toward him. He grabbed something out of his glove box and came back out of his car, spinning toward me, pointing the object from his glove box. It was a four-inch Colt Python held in his left hand.

"Stay where you are. I'm desperate, and I'll shoot if I have to."

I believed him. If there is anything worse than having a loaded gun pointed at you by a professional, it's having a loaded gun pointed at you by an amateur. A professional at least knows when he is going to pull the trigger, whereas an amateur can be stampeded by a provocation even he doesn't understand.

"Put that away, Professor. I'm not going to hurt you."

"You're not going to stop me, either." Blood was flowing out of Gault's nose into his mustache. There was more blood on his teeth and one eye was closing.

"Forget this nonsense. You should be back in your study researching Big Bill Haywood."

"They stole my son! I'm getting him back!"

"Alan, you're over-dramatizing," Helen told him from the corner of the building.

He looked her way, surprised that someone he knew

should be here. He shook his head as if he wanted to clear it. "No one is stopping me." Gault put the gun back on me. "Turn around. Get down on your knees."

I obeyed, bringing myself to face Wyckoff who had just managed to raise himself to one elbow. He made an effort to rise but failed and fell back. Behind me a motor started and tires spun on gravel. When I dared to glance over my shoulder, the Fiat was shooting down the alley toward Lorain Avenue. I got to my feet and stepped over to Helen, who was watching the Fiat disappear, shaking her head at the sight.

"I can't believe it. He's gone insane."

"Maybe it's like he says. He's desperate." Seeing that she was all right, I walked back over to Wyckoff and stood over him. He had managed to prop himself into a sitting position.

"Son of a bitch caught me when I wasn't looking. I'd'a taken him if you hadn't distracted me."

"Bullshit," I said. "You had plenty of time to put him away before I got here. You're going to have to learn to fight better than that or those pansies at Lucasville are going to ream your asshole raw."

Wyckoff was slow to grasp the implication. "Lucasville? The prison? What you saying?" He too had suffered damage in the fight. His right eyebrow was torn and he had a cut on his cheek that would develop into a scar.

"That's going to be your new home," I promised.

"What for?"

"Conspiracy to tamper with the scene of a crime." When you can't think of a law, make one up. "That's a heavy charge, good for ten or fifteen years."

"You got no proof of any such thing."

"I talked to Bobbie this afternoon. I saw her taking Monk's gun out of your apartment."

"You're a cop!" His tone made it an accusation.

"Not quite, which is the best thing going for you. If I had an arrest quota to meet, you'd be on your way to a cell in the Justice Center. The way it is, I have other interests. You answer my questions right and maybe we cut a deal."

He was sitting with his palms braced on the ground, my shadow lying heavy across his chest. "Let's hear it."

"John Monk. You knew him when you were growing up in Indiana?"

"Yeah. I got in some trouble when I was younger, kid stuff—a little pot, car theft, burglary. Monk helped me out instead of throwing the book at me. Like you."

"What did you do? Roll over on your buddies?"

"Hell, they left me hanging, so why not? They were adults when I was a juvie."

"Then when Monk set up his own detective agency, you went to work for him."

"Huh-uh. I never heard from him again until a couple weeks ago. Soon as I was old enough, I left Decatur and came to Cleveland."

"Why Cleveland?"

"My sister was living here. See, she used to work at this truck stop outside Fort Wayne. She met a driver who came from Cleveland and moved back here with him."

I ran my fingers along my jaw and heard a late afternoon rasp. "The guys you rolled over on were due to get out. That's why you left Decatur."

"Among other things."

"So how did you hitch up with Monk?"

"He kept track of people he knew, who owed him favors. He kept files on them, like a regular police department. When he had business in Cleveland, he looked me up."

"What kind of business?"

"The same scam he's been working lately, a baby snatch.

That was the kid's father you just chased off, if you didn't know that already. Monk needed my help and offered to make it worth my while."

"How did you help him?"

"Different ways. One thing, I helped on the snatch itself. We watched the kid's house in Cleveland Heights, waited until he was riding his bike to baseball practice last Wednesday, a week ago today. After we grabbed him, we took him to my apartment to hide him there. Just Monk and the kid. I had to clear out."

"Why was Monk using your apartment when he already had a motel room?"

"That's the way he operates. He wouldn't hold the kid in a motel room where he was registered. Cops might have traced him. Monk was careful."

"Not so careful he's still breathing. Who else was in on it?"

"No one."

"You lying shit!" I grabbed a handful of Wyckoff's shirt, pulled him to his feet, spun him around and shoved him against the brick wall of the body shop. "Lie to me again, asshole, and I'll really do a number on you. And this time it won't be love taps from a college professor."

Wyckoff stretched out his arms, palms up, to fend me off. "I didn't lie to you!"

"That's wrong. I know how Monk operated. He never pulled off a snatch without having the kid's relative along to take the heat."

"I don't know how he worked it other times. All I know is this time he din't." Wyckoff licked his lips as he grasped for an answer. "This time might have been different on account of the snatch was only a part of the plan. There was more to it."

I let Wyckoff see my anger subside so he would know I could be reasonable. "Tell me about that part."

"Besides getting the kid, he was supposed to prove that Gault, the father, did his wife down in Cincy when he was living there." Wyckoff came close to smiling as he watched my reaction to that bulletin. "Christ, you saw how he acted a few minutes ago. A wild man. The guy's gotta be a killer."

My mind was still trying to deal with Gault as a possible murderer of his wife. Was that the real basis of the animosity with his in-laws? "What did Monk have on him?" I asked Wyckoff.

"Don't I wish I knew. When I sent Bobbie to my apartment, I had her get the key to Monk's motel room. The reason for that was that Monk had a file on Gault in his briefcase. I wanted it so I could find out for myself. Then, I figured, I could pry some money outa Gault."

"The file is what you and Gault were fighting over when I showed up. The file that Gault grabbed before he took off."

Wyckoff bobbed his head. "Now you got it. I never had a chance to see everything. What I made out is that Gault had a woman on the side. He killed his wife and set it up so that it looked like a suicide. The police down there bought it, but Monk had some idea that the kid saw something. See, according to the reports, the kid found his mother's body, but Monk thought it happened different. He suspicioned that the kid might of walked in when his old man was strangling his mom. That's why he din't want any relatives around for the snatch, why he wanted time alone with the kid in my place. He figured he could play mind games with the kid, work some of his de-programmer tricks on him, get him to admit what he really saw."

"Or plant ideas in his head?"

"Well, shit, what difference does it make? Either way, we'd cinch the case against Gault. He'd still end up paying through the nose."

I got out my cigarettes and offered the pack to Wyckoff, a sign that we were buddies now. When we had lit up, I asked, "So what went wrong?"

"Someone killed Monk, that's what." Wyckoff inhaled deeply as if he were negating a bad taste in his mouth. "After we got the kid on Wednesday, I cleared out to let Monk operate. I stayed away all day Thursday and waited until late Friday before I dropped in. The kid is gone. Monk is dead. Man, I cleared out in a hurry. I stayed away all weekend and watched the news and read the paper, looking for word that Monk's body had been found. Nothing. I figure he won't be found until the stink gets so bad it can't be ignored. I start working on Bobbie to get her to go in there and pick up my things and also get the key to Monk's room."

"You also had her remove the Cobra."

"Huh?"

"The gun. The Colt Cobra."

"Yeah. See, I thought about the whole situation over the weekend and I doped it out. Whoever killed Monk tried to make it look like a suicide. He wouldn't of killed hisself. Why should he? I'll bet money it was Gault. So I think on it and I wonder, how can I screw him? Easy way is to move the gun. Right away the cops rule out suicide, see?"

"Did Gault know the Monk was in your apartment?"

"No." Wyckoff smiled crookedly, leading up to something. "But I doped that out, too. Say Monk got the kid to admit seeing Gault kill his mom. Now he's ready to put the squeeze on Gault. Monk calls him and says, come on over. You can have your son back and we'll talk cash. Gault comes and somewhere along the line, Monk gets careless. Gault gets hold of his gun and kills him, then rigs a suicide."

"In front of his son?"

Wyckoff shrugged. "What do the cops call it? The M.O.

Kill in front of the kid and fake a suicide. It worked for him before. Well, screw him. I took care of that by getting rid of the gun."

There were holes in his theory that needed plugging, but as long as it was the only theory in town, it was the best I had. From what I knew of Gault, I couldn't see him deliberately killing in front of his son. Aside from all other considerations, it's a poor technique to bring your own witness to observe your crimes. Besides, having seen the state that Gault was in, I knew I couldn't rule out anything. "Why did you come here?"

"My car's in there. Ernie lets me use the garage after hours so I can work on my transmission. Besides, I wanted someplace private to sit down and read Monk's report on Gault. Anyway, when I got here, Gault showed up. Maybe he'd been watching the place. We had words and he tried to take the file away from me. I guess I waved the file folder at him and said, like, 'I have proof you killed your wife.' So that made him want it worse and he came at me." Wyckoff flipped his cigarette away. "What happens now?"

"Up to you," I said. "I've still got the gun to give to the police if I have to."

Wyckoff was not happy with that development. He sauntered off to his sister's car, pausing every other step as if he expected me to stop him. I turned and walked over to the corner of the building where Helen had been standing, listening and watching. Now she wore the expression of a dyspeptic drama critic.

"Is that what you do all day when I'm not around?"

"Except when I have to get nasty and rough them up." I held the passenger door of my car for her, but Helen held back, studying me.

"There are sides of you I haven't seen." She got in then and I went around to the driver's side.

Before I started the car, I turned to her. "Most of the time the only thing I do is ask questions in quiet, conversational tones. Playing tough guy is a lousy technique, usually. Every once in a while, I run into a streetwise punk like Wyckoff who wouldn't give me the zit off his chin without a threat. Then my nice guy techniques are ruled out." The green Mustang went past on its way to the street. I started my own car then and turned it around to head away from Ernie's Body Shop. "If I couldn't be hard, I wouldn't be here. If I couldn't be gentle, I wouldn't deserve to be."

Helen seemed impressed with that at first. Before we reached the end of the block, she identified the source: "That sounds almost like Raymond Chandler."

IO

SILENCE HUNG like a lead ingot between us. I took Helen to dinner at a seafood restaurant near Kamm's Corners where I could practice eating without conversation. Amazing how fast you can get a meal down without gulping under those conditions, though it can seem like it's taking a long time. Near the end I told Helen I wanted to make a stop on our way home. I excused myself long enough to call Monica from the restaurant's pay phone. She snatched up the receiver on the first ring.

"What have you learned?" she gushed out as soon as I had identified myself.

"For one thing, Alan Gault is alive. I saw him briefly a little earlier."

"Thank God!"

"I need to explain the circumstances. It would go better in person. I could be at your place in fifteen minutes."

"Please come." She made it sound as if I would be doing her a favor to cross her threshold.

"One other thing. Helen Scagnetti will be with me, if you don't mind."

"Not at all."

I settled the bill with my Visa card and told Helen where we were going. She was as much company on the ride as my spare tire. From Kamm's Corners to Triskett was only a short jaunt, and Monica's address was only three blocks from the intersection, an apartment building in a series of identical places that had gone up in the building boom after World War II.

Monica was waiting for us at the door of her apartment. She shook hands with me and embraced Helen and invited us in. "Excuse the mess."

I looked for it but couldn't find it. The place was too neat to allow any dirt, except for what was in the potted house plants in macramé slings.

"Can I get you something?" Monica asked. "Tea? Coffee?"

We both accepted coffee and Monica rushed to her kitchen, returning in less than a minute with a service tray. She must have started to fix it when she hung up from our phone conversation.

"I suspected you would want coffee," Monica said to me. "You're observant."

That seemed to please her. Monica backed up and dropped to the front edge of a chair, triangulating herself with Helen and me, who sat at opposite ends of the couch. "Well?"

I plunged into it. "The most significant fact I've learned

today is that Brandon may have been kidnapped." I paused at that point and waited for Monica's reaction.

Behind her wide glasses, her eyes blinked rapidly for a space while she tried to process the information. "Kidnapped? But Professor Gault isn't rich. Who would do that?"

"A couple named Wesley and Esther Hammond who live in Fort Wayne. They were the parents of Gault's wife. Ransom has nothing to do with it. They seem to be convinced Gault is an unfit parent, so they want their grandson out of his control. They hired a man from Indianapolis named John Monk to do their dirty work."

Monica shook her head in disbelief. "From things Alan said, I knew his relations with his in-laws weren't good. Still, I can't believe they would do anything so—drastic. It's against the law, isn't it?"

"Basically, yes, but there are all kinds of complications. Ohio law provides an excuse for the parent who steals a child in the honest belief it's for the child's best interest. That can include grandparents. I don't know what Indiana law says, but you can bet that when two states get involved, things get three times as complex."

Monica turned to Helen with an expression that said: *Say it ain't so.*

Helen said, "What Gil is telling you is true."

"This man, John Monk, made his living off the loopholes in the law," I went on. "He was a professional at stealing children. It's why the Hammonds hired him."

Monica was close to tears of frustration. "They can't believe that Alan is an unfit parent. They have absolutely no proof."

"It's worse than that. They think Gault killed their daughter, Tricia."

Monica clapped both hands against the sides of her face. "That's not true! She killed herself."

"The Hammonds think that Brandon saw something that would prove Gault guilty. If Brandon is with them now, they might have convinced him he did."

"Good Lord!" Monica turned to Helen once more. "You know Alan. You know he could never harm anyone."

Helen had to look away. Her latest vision of Gault had been with a revolver in his hand and a wild look in his eye. "Everyone has dark places in his soul." She turned her head toward me. "Everyone is capable of the strangest things."

"It doesn't really matter," I said. "There's been another death. John Monk was shot last week and his body turned up today."

Monica was being hit by too many shocking developments in a short time. I nudged Helen and she went to Monica's side. She put an arm around Monica's shoulders and Monica began crying. Maybe I'd had a premonition about this scene coming up when I brought Helen along. In any case, it was a good moment for me to withdraw. I took my coffee cup into the kitchen where I found the percolator and treated myself to a refill. I also had a smoke while I was there, flicking my ashes into the sink and then drowning my cigarette under a spray of water.

When I returned, the women were ready for me. I had overheard some of Helen's words of comfort—depend on Gil, he'll know what to do. "What does it all mean?" Monica asked.

"I'm not sure. The answers aren't here. They might be in Fort Wayne. If you want me to find them, I'll have to go there."

"Of course." Monica agreed quickly.

"Not so fast. Going to Fort Wayne means running up the expense account—mileage, meals, a place to stay. Are you sure that's what you want?"

Monica stood up and strode across the room to a drop-leaf secretary from which she took her checkbook. "I told you I was willing to pay." She looked at her clock, which was showing 8:50. "Have you put in twelve hours today?"

Looking at the clock, I realized I had. How time flies when you're having fun. I said, "Ten honest hours would be more accurate." Two hundred dollars, double her retainer, I calculated.

Monica filled out the check, tore it off and handed it to me. Five hundred dollars. "Will that be sufficient for your trip?"

I looked at the check and then into Monica's eyes. "Do you understand what you're buying?"

"I want you to rescue Brandon and protect Alan," she said simply.

"If I rescue Brandon, it will be by legal means because I'm not in the baby-snatch business. Even if this gets to a court, I'm not sure Gault can win custody back. A court is likely to let Brandon stay with his grandparents."

"How could that be?"

"Gault can't put up much of a claim for being a fit parent if he's under indictment for murder." After giving Monica time to absorb the shock, I added, "I'm not judging what might have happened between Gault and his wife last year. No matter how that went, Gault is a strong suspect in Monk's murder last week."

Monica looked upset. "No. I don't believe it. Professor Gault could never kill anyone." She shook her head.

"If I go to Fort Wayne and stir up this mess, I might very well turn up evidence of Gault's guilt. If that happens, I go to the police with what I learn because I don't cover up murder cases. Which means you could very well be paying me to prove Gault guilty."

"Never. I can't believe a man as gentle as Alan is capable of murder." Her eyes seemed moist.

Arguing with her blind spot on that subject would have been a waste of time. I had said the things that would pamper my conscience, and now that they were on record I was satisfied. I wanted to go on with this case for no better reason than that I couldn't let myself quit without knowing the truth. "I'll put you on a daily rate while I'm traveling. You'll get a full statement when I get back." I put her check in my wallet.

"I'm not concerned with statements. Clear Alan's name and find Brandon. That will be reward enough."

"I can't promise that."

"I have confidence in you." She looked at Helen. "You have yourself a good man."

An endorsement like that was what I needed in the circumstances. Helen mumbled thanks and looked at me askew, as if she suspected I had arranged for it.

Outside, the interminable twilight of daylight saving time was still on the land. I drove Helen back up Lorain Avenue to the Burger Chef where her car still sat and waited until she had started it, allowing her to pull out ahead of me. Before I went home, I stopped at a bank and used my magic money card to deposit Monica's checks in my business account. When I reached Helen's house, her car was in the driveway and she was inside. I entered by the kitchen, girded for battle or the silent treatment, but she was waiting to rush into my arms.

We necked for a few minutes and Helen put her head on my shoulder. "I'll never understand you totally. I have to appreciate you for what you are."

"What is that?" I asked.

She leaned back in my arms to look into my eyes. "You really don't know, do you?"

"Would I ask you if I did?"

"No you wouldn't, and that's the point. You act. You never analyze. You see a problem and all you think about is what has to be *done*. Then you do it. Then you move on."

"My work's finished here, ma'm. Time to move on and clean up the next town. Like that?"

"Exactly." Helen laughed at the expression on my face. "See, right now you doubt me because you can't conceive of being any other way. But that's not the way it is with some people, with me. In the academic environment where I live, everything has to be discussed, to be thought through, to be analyzed to death."

"I'm supposed to get in touch with my feelings? Think about relationships? Start watching 'thirtysomething'?"

"It might not hurt."

"And the next time I read a book with those fat paragraphs that tell what someone is thinking, I'm supposed to actually read it instead of skimming over it?"

"You skim over introspection?"

"Always. Just like those scenes where they go into a restaurant and start telling you everything they had to eat."

"You're not supposed to do that. I see I have a lot to teach you."

"That has a lot to do with us—teaching, I mean. I'm a project for you, someone to be tutored, to be molded."

Helen thought it over. "There's a lot of truth in that. Teaching is my profession. I don't suppose I can turn it off any more than you can quit asking questions. Come to think of it, our professions aren't so far apart at that. We're both searching for truth and the solution to problems of human nature."

"That's heavy." I began turning off the downstairs lights.

"But I learn, too. I used to be afraid of guns until you taught me to shoot. Back then I thought that more laws were the answer until you convinced me otherwise. That's only one example of how we accommodate to one another. Take politics. You're conservative and I'm liberal, but we both can learn from one another because we have open minds. Don't you see? That's an important key to our life together. It's an adventure with both of us on a quest. Never finished, always becoming."

I took her hand and led her to the stairs. "Lecture's over."

A little later, when we were lying naked in bed and the sun had at last set, I had a suggestion for her. "Why don't you come with me to Fort Wayne tomorrow?"

"What would we do?"

"I can't be working all the time, and I'm going to have a very lonely motel room without you. We could stay there or go out and take in the culture of Indiana."

"Such as?"

"Cornfields. Johnny Appleseed's tomb. The Indy 500. The campus of Notre Dame."

Helen snuggled closer. "Don't I wish! Trouble is that besides all my classes, I have a faculty meeting I don't dare miss."

"Then you're going to have to make this a night to last me for a while."

"I'll see what I can do."

She managed it.

II

FIRST THING THURSDAY MORNING I called in to Moe Glickman's Bail Bonds to let Gladys know I would be out of town on a case for the next couple days. If anything came up needing me to track down a bail jumper, I wouldn't be available until Monday. Gladys told me Wally Stamm would handle things until I got back.

When I had seen Helen off to class, I packed a couple bags and put them in the trunk of my Caprice. I filled my travel mug with coffee and left the house. Before I got on the road, I stopped at the bank to withdraw two hundred dollars in expense money and then headed for the I-90 freeway. It carried me through the western suburbs—Lakewood, Rocky River, Bay Village—on toward the last outpost of urban sprawl that direction, the cities of Lorain and Elyria, where I connected with the Turnpike.

Despite all the jokes about it, Cleveland is an Eastern city at heart. Founded by New Englanders, it always looks east, anchoring one end of the American Saar that runs through Youngstown to Pittsburgh and beyond to the coal fields of West Virginia. In its glory days, when Rockefeller's oil and Carnegie's steel were its cornerstones, Cleveland kept up its ties to the East Coast. The influx of Central-European immigrants, who were funneled through Ellis Island, only added to its Eastern ties. Lately, film companies have been coming there for location shooting that allegedly takes place in New England. Cleveland is the last outpost before the Midwest begins.

Cruise control set at sixty-five, radio tuned to the newstalk station, air conditioner chilling the interior, sipping coffee from my travel mug, I glided across the glacial planes of northern Ohio. Beyond the megalopolis, there was nothing to see but land so level that pitcher's mound at the local high school field marked the highest point in the county. The sight of all that emptiness, as it always does, made me vaguely uneasy with the realization of how little of this planet is actually inhabited. No streets, no curbs, no sewer system, houses spaced so far apart your neighbor's place is out of sight. Four hundred years after this continent was discovered, man's impression on the landscape barely amounts to a toehold. All the houses and commercial buildings, all the highways and railroads, all the cars and people gathered together and dumped in one spot wouldn't fill one Eastern state. It was a humbling concept.

By noon I was passing the exits for Toledo, although there was no sign of a major city anywhere. Thirty miles past it, I stopped at one of the turnpike plazas to replenish my coffee supply and get a couple of take-out burgers. An hour later I crossed the Indiana border by passing through a set of gates that converted the Ohio Turnpike into the Indiana Toll Road. It looked like a continuation of Ohio to me. A little over ten miles of that brought me to the intersection with Interstate 69, fifty miles north of Fort Wayne. I started south on the last leg to my destination. My route may not have been the most direct, but it had kept me on super highway, off two-lane blacktop.

On the outskirts of Fort Wayne, I found a convenient parking lot and fished a motel directory out of the clutter of my backseat to find a place that would accept my credit card. Next stop was a drug store to pick up a Fort Wayne street guide that would lead me to my chosen motel. It was just off the Interstate at the intersection of Goshen Road and Coliseum Boulevard, the kind of place a budget range of twenty-five to thirty dollars a night will allow. When I had registered, I went to my room off the second-floor balcony where I hung up my suitbag and set my suitcase down, turned on the air-conditioning, and used the phone book to find an address for Wesley Hammond on Glenwood Avenue. Back to my street guide to get a fix on his house and dope out a route to it from my motel.

The afternoon was already waning, but I had gained an hour crossing the state line, and in any case, I was in no hurry. If the Hammonds did have Brandon, I wanted to hit them when the kid was sure to be there. Dinner time would be ideal, leaving me a good hour to kill. I decided I could squander it over a meal and started out to find a restaurant. At the door, something hit me and I turned back for a last look at my room. Déjà vu. But why? And then it came to me. The room with my suitbag hanging and my suitcase sitting, with my street guide out, was a nearly perfect replication of

Monk John's room at the Dreamland in Cleveland. Maybe we were closer than I had ever realized.

With a meal behind my belt buckle, I headed east on Coliseum past the Fort Wayne campus of Purdue University and the burial site of Johnny Appleseed, then south on Hobson to my destination. It was in a residential neighborhood developed maybe twenty-five years ago when it would have been teeming with children. Now those children were grown and had moved away to establish homes of their own, the swing sets had been dismantled, the trees had grown larger, and the houses were only half filled. The Hammond house was the same basic ranch as its neighbors with a second-floor addition with dormer windows at the back. I parked across the street in the shade of a maple tree and got out. Windows were up in the nearest house, bringing me Dan Rather's voice explaining something about Saudi Arabia. There was a sign in the front window of the Hammond house: DON'T WORRY ABOUT THE DOG—WATCH OUT FOR THE OWNER, with the drawing of a hand holding a revolver. The inner door was open, but the aluminum screen door, a script H worked into its frame, was latched. I rang the bell.

She appeared in the doorway without any warning she was approaching, no sound and no sight. The doorway was empty and then she was standing in it, an open Bible pressed against her breast. "Whom were you seeking?"

"Wesley Hammond," I answered respectfully.

"My husband is not here. He has gone to a baseball game." There was a hum of disapproval in her voice.

Never date a girl until you see her mother because that is what she will look like in twenty years, my folks had advised me when I was a randy youth. Having seen Arlene Hammond yesterday, I tried to apply the advice in reverse, to see if I could imagine this woman siring a future centerfold. It seemed unlikely until I looked beyond her plain face to the bone structure beneath it. If Esther Hammond had ever taken the basic care or applied even a minimum of makeup, she might have been a comely woman. To reach the washed-out, wrinkled state I saw had taken half a century of neglect. Her hair was drawn into a bun tight enough to raise her eyebrows an inch.

"Where? Cincinnati? Detroit? Chicago?"

She shook her head with benign tolerance. "None of those sinful professional games. They distract people from more important things and besides, they play on the Lord's day."

Verily, verily I say unto you, these words have been spoken to one who considers baseball a sacrament. "Then where did he go?"

"To the local field." She took a hand off her Bible to point the way. "If you go down Carew two blocks, you will see it."

I thanked her and got back in my car, following her directions, trying to recall if Fort Wayne had a Class C franchise. Carew Street simply dead-ended into the parking lot at a playground, with tennis courts on my left and a picnic area ahead. A Little League field was on my right. I parked in the gravel lot and walked up to the game in progress. The few bleacher seats behind home plate were already taken with the overflow in lawn chairs along the base paths. I stood between the refreshment stand and the third-base dugout, actually a bench on the spectator side of the fence. The team using that dugout was at bat, so the bench was full. I maneuvered my way to the end of the bench to look down the line at the players' faces. There were at least four tow-headed kids who could have been Brandon. The uniforms they wore made them look even more alike.

I turned to the team on the field and counted southpaws. First base, pitcher, left fielder. The first baseman was too tall

and too dark. The pitcher was a question mark. The left
fielder, the one nearest me, was about the right size and had
blond hair. As I watched, the batter drove a grounder between short and third into left. Instead of charging the ball,
the fielder waited for it to come to him, and then made only a
halfhearted effort to bend down for it before it went through
his legs like a croquet wicket. Even by Little League standards, it was a bad performance.

Spectators groaned in the stands along the first base line. I
scanned the crowd. Parents of that age group were well
under forty, making it easy to spot the grandparents who
were a generation older. I was looking for one who might
have been a deputy sheriff. A couple were easy to elimin-
ate because they were too short ever to have qualified. I settled for a beefy man with white hair clipped so short it was
little more than beard stubble, thin enough to show sun-
burned scalp. He was shaking his head in disgust at the left
fielder's error. He would be Hammond to me until I learned
different.

By the time the inning ended, I had worked my way to the
first base side where I could watch the players come in. Close
up, I eliminated the pitcher and kept my eye on the left
fielder. He walked while the manager yelled, "Hustle! Hustle!" At the dugout bench, he went to the most remote end,
dropped his glove behind him, and sat staring at his Astro-
turf spikes. I contrived to pass along the back of the bench on
my way to the refreshment stand so I could get a look at the
left fielder's glove. Along the back of the middle finger someone had printed a name in Magic Marker: BRANDON G.

Like most Little League games, this one was interminable.
Pitching, wild as it was, was far ahead of hitting. Batters took
their place in the box and ran up a 3–2 count nearly every
time. Then they struck out or walked or got hit by a pitch.

The few that made contact dribbled grounders to the infield and got on base about half the time through errors. When I returned from the refreshment stand, Brandon was coming into the on-deck circle. He simply waited there, not taking practice swings, not gauging the pitcher's speed, holding an aluminum bat like a guidon bearer. His turn came and he stepped into the portside batter's box, resting the bat on his shoulder, barely looking toward the mound. The pitches went by him. Ball. Strike. Ball. Ball. Strike. With a 3–2 count, the pitcher floated a luscious strike across the heart of the plate. Brandon watched it go by. He went back to the dugout to turn in his helmet and bat.

In the stands, Hammond was again shaking his head. I was puzzled, too. Everything I had heard about Brandon led me to believe he was a good and enthusiastic player. This kid was dogging it as bad as I had ever seen, as if the diamond were the last place in the world he wanted to be.

Brandon stood in the outfield two more innings without a ball coming his way. He came to bat once more. This time the pitcher was wise enough to waste no energy on him. He simply lobbed three balls through the strike zone and Brandon took them all. That made a total of nine pitches without one swing. This time when Brandon sat down, the manager spoke to him a few minutes. When the team took the field again, Brandon stayed on the bench. He studied his shoes for the rest of the game.

After the last out, I moseyed over by the dugout as Hammond headed that way to claim Brandon. I managed to eavesdrop on some of the conversation: the manager saying Brandon had to put out more effort. Hammond saying Brandon was going through a period of adjustment to his new home. Hammond expressing gratitude to the league for allowing Brandon to play at all on this pick-up team of late arrivals. Hammond left at last, walking with his arm around Brandon's shoulders over to the concession stand for a treat.

They were drinking Cokes there when I caught up with them. "Say, aren't you Wes Hammond?" I asked.

He turned to see who was addressing him. "That's right." I handed him one of my cards. He looked at it and frowned. "Private detective? From Cleveland?" He looked from my card to me. "What do you want?"

I inclined my head to Brandon, not wanting to be too explicit in front of him. "Did you really think you could get away with this? After all those years you put on the sheriff's department?"

"We've got him." Hammond's eyes measured and evaluated me. We were the same height, but he was heavier and more muscular, despite the years he conceded. "Think you can change that?"

"I wouldn't even try, not that way. It would put me in the same class as John Monk."

His only reaction to the name was a couple of rapid blinks. "Then tell Gault to hire his lawyers and hunker down for a long battle. The thing is, he won't want to bother when he realizes what he's facing."

"You're talking about the old scandal in Cincinnati."

He shook his head. "I'm talking about the new scandal in Cleveland."

My face must have shown more than I intended. Hammond smiled. "How long you been on the case, son?"

"This is my second day."

"So you really don't know what you're dealing with. I think I better fill you in. Got a car? Good. Brandon and I walked here, so you can give us a ride home. How does that sound, Brandon?"

"All right." He sipped his Coke.

I led them to my car, mystified by Hammond's attitude. He was exuding confidence to a degree that made me cautious. I suspected he knew something I didn't.

"Nice car, isn't it?" Hammond asked.

"It's all right," Brandon answered.

"Ought to have seatbelts, though. We got a law here that says you hafta use them. Not that anyone pays attention to it. You used to be a cop, right?"

"A couple years."

"Ever see an accident where someone was saved by a seatbelt?"

"No."

"Ever see one where someone was saved by not having a belt on?"

"A couple hundred maybe."

"Same here, only I was at it longer, so I saw more. Fuckers in Washington say the states have to pass laws to try to protect us from ourselves. All the law does is take away your freedom of choice. You own guns, don't you?"

"A few."

"How many are registered?"

"None."

"Same here."

By this time we were approaching his house. I stopped in his driveway but Hammond made no move to get out. Instead, he turned to Brandon in the backseat. "Go in the house and tell Grandma I've got some business with this man. We're going to drive around awhile and discuss it. Got all that?"

"Yes, Grandpa," Brandon said listlessly.

Hammond watched him trudge up the driveway to the house, waiting until he had actually gone inside before he spoke. "Nice kid."

"Doesn't seem very active," I pointed out.

"Catatonic, the doctors call it. Good thing we got him when we did or Gault would have turned him into a complete faggot." Hammond looked away from his house back to me. "Let's roll. I'll show you where to go so I can tell you what a load of shit you've stepped in."

12

HAMMOND DIRECTED ME through the streets of tract homes to Anthony Boulevard, then left to the next main drag, which was State. Half a block from the intersection was a neighborhood watering hole with knotty pine walls and scarred furnishings. Half a dozen regular customers spoke to him as he made his way to the back booth and ordered a pitcher of beer and two glasses. He avoided any significant conversation until we were served.

"I heard awhile back that the Cleveland Police Department was thinking of going to 9mm automatics. Anything ever come of it?"

"They're still using Model 10 Smiths," I told him.

"You in favor of the change?"

"I wouldn't mind switching to an automatic, but I'm not wild about the caliber. Nine millimeter is just a .38 Special under another name with all the problems a .38 has with stopping power. Plus a nine penetrates too much for use in an urban area."

"Damned right!" He seemed pleased with my answer, as if I had passed a test. "What would you go for, then? Colt .45?"

"That's my first choice. Maybe the Bren Ten or that new Smith & Wesson .45 in double action. I'm not wild about double action in an automatic, but I can live with it."

Our pitcher of beer arrived. I paid for it and Hammond poured. "The wife doesn't want me having this around the house, so I do my drinking away from home." He drained half his glass on first swallow and refilled, ready for business now. "I wonder how much you know already. You know I hired John Monk to snatch Brandon for us."

"I found his body."

"No you didn't." Hammond tapped a forefinger with a chewed nail against his own chest. "I did, last Friday when he was still fresh."

I lit a cigarette and nodded. "He sure wasn't fresh when I found him yesterday."

"I used to know John Monk when he was a deputy here in Allen County, a juvenile officer. Then he quit and moved to Indianapolis. There was a reason for that." Hammond picked up his beer and sipped it. "The Monk was in his glory while he was a kiddy cop. He really liked the kids. He could relate to them. He really related sometimes."

I picked up on his hints. "You're saying he was a pederast."

"No, he was a pervert who went for the young stuff, boys and girls both. He was careful about it, and the ones he dealt with weren't about to complain. Half of them were willing and the other half went along because it was keeping them out of trouble. None of which stopped rumors from circulating, and finally Monk decided it was better to resign." Hammond picked up the pitcher. "Ready for more?"

"I'm fine." My beer had been barely touched.

"When Monk started on his own, the big thing was the de-programmer business. He'd sneak into one of those religious communes and snatch the kid, take the kid to a motel room, and spend a couple days brainwashing the kid back to real life. That suited Monk fine, locked in a motel room with the kid for a couple days. Who knows what went on then? That business fell on hard times after a couple years, so Monk put his talents to work in another direction. He went in for parental abductions, most of them coming out of custody disputes in divorce cases. It's the big thing now, right? Pictures on milk cartons and all that? So Monk is milking the trend. That doesn't mean he's not good at what he does. Hell, that's why I turned to him when I needed help." Hammond looked away. "I thought he'd have some standards, that he'd be professional enough to leave off that other stuff."

I sipped some of my unwanted beer. "Besides getting Brandon back, you wanted more from Monk."

"Damned right! Gault killed my daughter in Cincinnati, plain and simple, and he was getting away with it. Can you blame me for wanting that fixed?"

"No way."

"But you're working for Gault. Don't it bother you that the man who signs your checks snuffed his wife?"

"I'm not working for Gault. I'm working for people who hired me to find him and Brandon, on the assumption they would be together. Besides, it doesn't matter what Gault might have done. I'm out to get the facts. If someone asks me to find out what color shorts you wear, that's what I do. It doesn't matter if they're white or polka dot. I report the truth."

Hammond patted his palms in a noiseless applause. "Very noble."

"It's also good business in the long run. Why did you hire Monk anyway? You have the moxie to do it yourself."

"Rule One is that you don't investigate a case you're emotionally involved in. On top of that, if I did turn up evidence that Gault murdered my daughter, the first accusation they would make is that I manufactured it. Best thing was to let someone else do it."

Let Monk manufacture the evidence? I clamped my teeth together to keep from saying that aloud. "He do you any good?"

"Instead of going direct to Cleveland, he was scheduled to spend some time in Cincinnati. I guess he did, but I never got a report on what he found."

"Who was he supposed to see?"

"The starting place was the police department—Sergeant Gilmore in Homicide. He's a coon but a sharp one. Where Monk went from there, I wouldn't know."

But I had some clues, geographically speaking, by the marks on his map. "You must have had something to make you suspicious of Gault in the first place."

"Lots of them." He began counting on his fingers. "Tricia's insurance money, two hundred grand. Gault's character, which doesn't need much more. Tricia's religious beliefs, which teach she would go to hell without a chance of redemption for killing herself. Gault keeping another woman on the side. Tricia being against divorce. Mix it all together, and you've got a motive for murder."

"There's a difference between proving motive and proving the act."

"Small step."

"You're sure Gault was playing around?"

"Common knowledge. Hell, Tricia knew it. She's the one who told us six months before she died."

"None of which proves Gault slipped a rope around her neck."

Hammond primed himself with more beer before he reached into his bag for the *coup de grace*. "At the time of Tricia's funeral, Esther and me went to Cincinnati for a few days. Esther spent most of her time taking care of Brandon. She thought it would be a good idea to get him to talk about it, thinking all he had done was find the body. She got him to draw pictures—simple things, like a house with a figure for his mother down in the basement and another figure representing Brandon coming in the door. Then I noticed that every time he tried to draw the scene, there was a third figure in the house. We realized what it meant. When Brandon came home from school and found Tricia's body, someone else was there."

Hammond paused to give me time to absorb the import of his words. I failed to shout "Huzzah!" or turn handsprings. Instead, I reached for another Camel. "Brandon told her who it was?"

"No. He refused to talk about it, just clammed up completely. We think it was a man from his drawings, but that's not even sure. The truth isn't hard to see. The man was Brandon's own father. He knows that up here." Hammond tapped a forefinger against his temple. "He's blocking it out, as the shrinks say. Get Brandon to admit to what he saw and you'll have Gault riding the lightning. It explains why Gault took Brandon and went off to Cleveland—to get away from Esther and me."

"What kind of alibi did Gault have for the time of Tricia's death?"

"He was between classes and went to the library to do some research. People saw him go in the stacks. No one saw him sneak out, but that doesn't mean he couldn't have. He could have made it home in time to do the job and get back for his next lecture."

"Thin," I noted.

"We could have filled in the blanks given more time with Brandon. That's what Monk was trying to buy us in Cleveland. He arranged to use an apartment down in the part of town where the Polacks live so he could have some time alone with Brandon. It sounded good to me, but I was only thinking about Monk using his de-programmer techniques to break down Brandon's mental block." Hammond shook his head in regret. "Mental block, shit. I had the biggest one of all. I shoulda known better than to trust Monk with a kid but I couldn't see it."

"You mean—"

"He butt-fucked Brandon. First thing we noticed when we got him back was blood in his stool. We took him to a doctor who had to give him a couple stitches. Fucking perverted bastard! And I'm the dumbass that set it up for him." Hammond drank more beer and poured more, adding an inch to my glass. "You're falling behind."

"You still haven't told me how you found Monk's body." Even as I said that much, I wondered if *found* was the appropriate word.

"Guess I've been putting it off." Hammond rolled his glass between his palms, watching the beer. "Thursday afternoon, week ago today, we got a call from Monk. He told us where he was and gave us directions for getting there. Said to come tomorrow and pick up the kid. That was too long for Esther. We started out Thursday and drove as far as Mansfield, where we got a room for the night. Friday morning we drove the rest of the way to Cleveland and got to the place around nine-thirty. Knocked. No answer. Maybe they had gone out for breakfast. We tried again around 10:15. Still no answer. By noon I figured something serious was wrong. I shimmed the door and went in. That's how we found them."

"Tell me."

He shrugged. "You saw it, didn't you? Monk in the chair with a bullet hole in his face. Brandon was in the bathroom huddled up in the tub, crying. You see what he's like now, doesn't give a damn one way or the other. It's not like him but under the circumstances, it's what you got to expect."

"Because Brandon witnessed Monk kill himself?"

"No such thing. It wasn't suicide."

Like a karate chop through my heart, the impact of what Hammond was telling me hit home. "You can't mean that."

"You dense?" Hammond's voice had risen, suppressed anger erupting after a week of silence. He lowered his voice to a tone that nearly hissed the words at me. "There were only two people locked in that apartment. One of them ends up dead. How many suspects you got left?"

"Brandon—"

"—was taken to the apartment by Monk. Monk plays with his mind. Boogers him. Brandon is hurt and mad at Monk. He gets hold of Monk's Cobra. Walks up to the chair where Monk is sitting. Maybe Monk laughs at him. Maybe he grabs for the gun. *Bang!* It's done."

We stared at one another across the table. The words had been spoken. Nothing was ever going to erase them.

Hammond broke the spell by taking one deep breath. "When I had looked over the situation, I picked up Monk's Cobra from the bathroom floor by the hammer and carried it into the living room and dropped it near his chair. It wasn't a perfect frame for suicide, but good enough to confuse the local law. We checked to make sure there was no trace of

Brandon and hustled him out of there before anyone saw us. We brought him back to Fort Wayne and here he stays. Whatever happens next, Brandon is going to need a lot of tender loving care from us. And Gault isn't going to cause any trouble, unless he wants the world to know his son is a killer. You see him, you tell him that."

"Gault will know you're bluffing. You would never put Brandon on that kind of spot."

"Don't be so sure. Would that be any worse than letting him live with a murderer like Gault? A man who has already killed his son's mother? You don't want to push me on this one."

Hammond's face held a totally incongruous smile that told me better than any words how serious he was. He had become a true believer, who would crash a carload of explosives into a building to prove a point, the kind of man who prefers nuclear winter to negotiation. He looked up at the clock over the bar. "Time to be getting back to the little woman."

We left our booth and went out to my car. I drove through the residential streets, stopping when I got to Glenwood to let a taxi go by. The passenger seat was empty. I turned onto the street and went to Hammond's house and turned once more into his driveway. He had his door open and one foot on the blacktop when the sound of loud voices from inside the house reached us. The words were indistinguishable, but the sound of anger could not have been plainer. Hammond frowned and got out without saying a word, heading for his front door. I followed a couple steps behind, catching his screen door after him before it could swing shut.

"You are not welcome under this roof," Esther Hammond's voice was saying. "My prayers for you have failed while you continue in your sin."

"That's rich. I don't need lectures on my sinful nature from a criminal," another female voice shot back.

"How dare you!"

"Criminal," she repeated. "Kidnapper. You have Brandon with you at this very moment."

I was just entering the house behind Hammond, his bulk blocking my view. One more step and I could see around him. Esther Hammond, her Bible pressed against her breast, was standing before an oval copy of Sallman's *Head of Christ*, facing her opponent, whose back was to me.

The noise Hammond and I made entering caused the opponent to turn her head, showing me a face that had once looked out from a magazine page above a body without clothes.

Arlene.

13

"ARLENE!" Thus Hammond proved he could recognize his own daughter no matter how unwelcome she was. In a voice not entirely lacking affection, he added, "What the hell are you doing here?"

"Trying to protect you, believe it or not," she answered in a voice a few ranges lower than it had been.

Hammond held out his arms and Arlene stepped into them to receive a hug. Esther watched the action with an expression that could have portrayed jealousy. Behind Hammond, I saw Arlene's arms go around his neck and back, her fingers loaded with rings, her arms clanking bracelets. After a few seconds of the embrace, Arlene opened her eyes and saw me over her father's shoulder.

"You? Here?"

I shrugged. "Call me peripatetic."

Arlene pushed away from her father, the interlude of affection over and Round Two about to begin.

"Wesley, I want that piece of trash out of my house," Esther demanded. "You should be ashamed of yourself hugging her to you. Her body is probably wracked with all sorts of evil diseases."

"Now Esther—" Hammond said soothingly as he stepped toward his wife.

"There is no room for her here," Esther insisted. "She is a harlot."

"You shouldn't read your Bible so selectively, Mom," Arlene told her. "What about the story where Jesus told them off. 'Let the one without sin cast the first stone.' I don't see anyone in here capable of picking up a rock."

I was advancing toward Arlene. Hammond and I, ex-cops, were instinctively handling this like a family disturbance call. We were interposing ourselves, going one-on-one with the combatants to separate them.

"How dare she quote Scripture to me?"

"Seems to me," I said, "Jesus was never offended by fallen women. He had a ladies' auxiliary made up of prostitutes."

"The devil can quote Scripture to his own purpose," Esther reminded me.

"Thanks for the endorsement," Arlene said in a sarcastic undertone.

"Not that Arlene should be classed with them," I added hastily.

"Whatever you think of Arlene," Hammond was saying to his wife, "she's still our daughter as much as Tricia was. So why don't we try sitting down and getting calm."

He guided his wife to a rocking chair, while I steered

Arlene to a ladder-back chair diagonally across the room. Neutral corners. Today Arlene wore a simple blue summer dress that matched her eyes when they flashed with anger and that rose and fell as her breast moved with her agitated breathing.

"How did you get here?" I asked conversationally.

"I flew out." Her heaving breasts subsided slightly as she came down from her peak of anger. "After I talked to you yesterday, I stewed about what was happening. I had to find out if Brandon was here. All the way I kept telling myself they wouldn't be foolish enough to steal him." Her anger was starting to rise again now as she recalled the incident. "Then I walked in the door and there he was."

"I know."

"Brandon is in good hands with us," Esther put in behind me. "You say you don't even know where Alan Gault is. How can he be a good father when he's nowhere to be found."

"She has a point," I said.

"Are you on their side?" Arlene asked me.

"I'm on Brandon's side."

She ran her fingers through a loose shock of hair and looked at her mother. I turned, too, and saw her sitting in the chair with her Bible in her lap, the first time it had not been held against her chest. Esther was every bit as well-developed as her daughter. I realized she made a habit of holding her Bible there to conceal her breasts, to abject herself, to hide her desirability from men.

"Don't you realize what you have done?" Arlene was asking. "It's a serious crime. You could go to prison for many years."

"A fraction of the time Alan Gault should spend for what he has done," said Esther. "Perhaps we can be cell mates."

There was a fireplace at one end of the room, I noted, with a photo of a woman hung up on the chimney. I recognized Tricia from the painting I had seen in Gault's house in Cleveland Heights. This photo had been taken in Kodacolor, but the effect was strangely similar to the painting. The background had been neutral and Tricia's flesh tones again tended to blend into it. Every visible article of clothing was a pastel shade that tended to bleed into its neighbor, giving the impression of a monochrome with no distinguishing features. From that photo and others around the room, Tricia seemed to look at us with bland detachment. There were no pictures of Arlene.

"You know I'm not a criminal," her father reasoned. "I spent my life fighting crime. I'm willing to go into any court any time and justify what I've done to a jury. I won't be surprised if they find in my favor. Grandparents have rights, too. The point of all this is that I'll never get there unless Gault files the complaint, which so far he isn't doing, and which I have reason for knowing he never will. In any case, you're not the one to start the process. You have no interest in it."

"It's still not right," Arlene insisted, devoid of any other argument.

"God's will is the final authority. You should learn to submit to it," Esther advised.

"I won't submit to the will of any god that sanctions stealing children," Arlene shot back.

"Wesley, really! Our home cannot be blessed if we permit such blasphemy under our roof."

Hammond still wanted to make peace between his women. "Arlene, can't you keep your atheistic beliefs to yourself while you're in our house?"

"Meaning I should quit pointing out your stupidity. Before I quit that, I'll leave." Arlene stood up. "Let me use your phone to call a cab."

"Don't bother," I said. "I'll give you a ride wherever you need to go."

Arlene picked up her purse and an overnight bag twice the size of the purse. She hooked its strap over her shoulder like a rifle sling, jingling bracelets in the silence on her way to the door. Her parting words were addressed to me: "I'll wait in your car."

I stayed behind only long enough to give Hammond another one of my cards. This time I wrote my home phone number on it and the name of my motel. While I was doing that, Brandon came out of another room to look questioningly at us adults. He had changed from his Little League uniform into a Cincinnati Reds T-shirt and a pair of jeans.

"Where's Aunt Arlene?" he asked.

"She had to leave already," Esther told him.

Handing my card to Hammond, I said, "Let me know the minute you hear from Gault."

"Right. You going back to Cleveland tomorrow?"

"Cincinnati first. I don't know where I'll be staying there. Reach me through Sergeant Gilmore, I guess."

"Aunt Arlene always gives me a present," Brandon complained with a child's unabashed greed.

While Brandon's grandparents studied their wallpaper, I fished a dollar out of my pocket and gave it to him. "Arlene gave this to me so I could give it to you. She said to buy yourself something you wouldn't get otherwise."

When no one objected, Brandon reached for the money. I held it away from him. "One thing first. Promise you'll show some hustle next game, all right?"

"All right," Brandon agreed.

I parted with the buck and went out to my car. Arlene was sitting on the passenger side of the front seat, dabbing her eyes with a Kleenex. I backed out of the driveway and went down Glenwood. Two blocks away, Arlene was ready to talk.

"Why does it always have to be like that? Why can't I just have a visit with my parents like normal people?" She brooded over that question for a while. "Can you believe that was the most sensible visit I've had in years? Your being there had a lot to do with that. I guess you aren't a grad student after all."

"Not quite." I passed her the folder that held my ID card. She read it and gave it back to me.

"I don't get it. What's your interest in all this?"

"Monica Brodbeck hired me to find Gault. She was worried when he and Brandon disappeared."

"Brandon's tutor?" Arlene thought that over. "Of course she would. She's in love with Alan and she resents me."

I had driven far enough from Hammond's home that soon I would have to start choosing a destination. "Where did you want to go?"

"Any motel where I can get a room for the night. What I'd really like is a drink. But I don't want to go to a bar. I must be a fright." She moved my rear-view mirror to study her streaked mascara.

We were on Coliseum Boulevard now. I cruised along until I spotted a liquor store and turned into its parking lot, leaving Arlene long enough to dash inside to purchase a pint of Seagram's. Back in the car, I drove to my motel. This far west, it really was the land of the midnight sun. Only now, approaching ten o'clock Indiana time, was it getting dark enough to require headlights and see neon signs come on. I turned into my motel and parked below the balcony under my door.

"What do you have in mind?" Arlene asked, staying in her seat.

"You're welcome to use my room to freshen up. Then you can have your drink. Then we can check with the desk to get you a room of your own."

"That's all?"

"I have a fulfilling sex life back home."

On that understanding she got her travel bag and allowed me to admit her. While she made use of my bathroom, I carried the plastic ice bucket down to the ice machine and filled it. When I returned to my room, Arlene was smoking and twisting the television dial.

"There are some things you don't notice until you've been away for a time," she remarked, "things we don't get in Cleveland. Preachers on every other channel and fertilizer commercials." She snapped off the set.

"Should I get you soda?"

"Water is fine."

I mixed a drink in a motel glass, added ice, and gave it to her for the test. She approved. I did it again for myself and sat down on the foot of my bed, letting her have the table. I tasted my drink, wondering again how anybody could develop a liking for the stuff.

Arlene had been watching me. "You're not used to doing this."

"Not as a rule. Today I've gone wild. I had part of a glass of beer with your father and now this. Tomorrow I'll probably wake up in a drunk tank with the DTs."

"I thought all private eyes were big drinkers."

"Sorry to disappoint." I put my drink aside and lit a cigarette. "I saw Gault yesterday."

She halted her glass an inch from her lips. "You did? Where?"

"On Lorain Avenue in Cleveland. He was duking it out with another guy in an alley."

"Alan? Fighting? That's hard to believe."

"When I tried to break it up, Gault pulled a gun on me and got out of there. He was babbling things about his son being held. I tried to reason with him but he wasn't having any."

Arlene sipped her drink in thought. When she put it down, she said, "Alan must be half out of his mind with worry. He must be running all over trying to find Brandon."

"Where Gault was wasn't very far from Lakewood. He didn't come to your place by any chance?"

She looked squarely at me. "I haven't seen him since I talked to you." If I had known her better, I might have been able to tell she was lying.

"It couldn't be that Gault put you up to coming out here to see if your parents have Brandon?"

"It was my own idea. I told you yesterday what I suspected."

"The reason I asked is that there's no flight to Fort Wayne out of Hopkins."

She took too long coming up with an answer. "I took a commuter flight to Toledo and made connections there."

"I was wrong. There is a direct flight from Burke Lakefront," I said.

Arlene's blue eyes had a fluorescent glow. "Do you want to see my ticket?"

"Only if you have one to show me."

"I discarded it at the airport." She stabbed out her cigarette in an ashtray, bracelets jingling with the effort. "What difference would it make if I crawled out here on my hands and knees?"

"It would make a lot of difference if you drove out here because Gault sent you. It would mean you've been in contact with him. It would mean you know more than you're telling."

Arlene sat staring at me, giving nothing away.

"It would mean," I added, "that you would know what Gault's been up to this last week. That might come in handy later when he needs an alibi."

"For what?"

"A man died in Cleveland during that time. John Monk. It looks like murder."

"The baby stealer I told you about yesterday?"

"He's the one who actually grabbed Brandon. Then he was shot. The Homicide detective I talked to is really anxious to have a chat with Gault."

She shook her head in disbelief, a gesture that made her her father's daughter. "Alan wouldn't kill anyone no matter what my parents think."

"A few minutes ago you didn't think he would get in a fistfight." I picked up her glass, mixed another drink for her, and brought it back. "If you really want to patch up affairs with your family, try working through your father. He has potential."

She looked at me afresh, the anger gone from her eyes. "The two of you hit it off, didn't you?"

"I wouldn't go that far. Your father turned out to be a more reasonable man than you led me to believe. He really has Brandon's best interests at heart. Plus the kid's done some things Gault should know about."

"Like what?"

"It's for Gault to know."

Arlene didn't press it. She finished her second drink and rolled her glass between her palms, another habit that showed her genetic links with Hammond. In her case her fingers were not only decorated with too many rings but came with long, slender fingers with long nails tinted pink. At last she said, "You're right about Dad. Without Mom, he's usually reasonable. It's Mom I have to keep trying to win over. Know what? I'm always giving her things, all sorts of presents, prizes from the sponsors at the stations I deal with. That's backwards. It's supposed to be the parent that tries to buy the child's love with presents."

Watching her, I was becoming conscious that I was alone in a motel room with a woman attractive enough to pose for nude art. For my own benefit, I said, "It's getting late. We'd better see about checking you into a room."

She might not have heard me. When she did react two beats later, it was as if the sound of my voice had reminded her I was in the room. "You're a strange man."

"You're not the first to make that observation."

"I was thinking that you landed in the middle of this whole mess but you keep forging ahead, doing the right things, restoring order where you can."

"I'm being paid for it." I picked up her bag. "Time to check in before all the rooms are gone."

Arlene stood up and started for the door, then stopped and turned to face me. "I've never thanked you for all you're doing."

"I said I'm being paid."

She stepped forward, slid her arms around my neck and kissed me. It wasn't much more than a peck, but when she stepped back her long lashes were low over her eyes.

"We were on our way to the desk," I noted.

"On second thought, it's foolish for both of us to pay for separate rooms when there's space for two in here. Want to split expenses?"

There was a part of me that cautioned it was time to get her out of here. There was another part delivering an entirely different message. Arlene was appealing to one of them. She turned away from the door and slowly sat down on the foot of my bed.

She raised her head and took a deep breath. "I'm being hit from too many different directions. My family. Alan. Brandon."

The sight of her sitting on my bed evoked images of how she must have looked in her centerfold appearance. I put her suitcase on the floor. Well, there was no use in holding it forever.

"I envy you. You must have such a stable home life." She put her hands flat on the counterpane behind her and leaned back, a position that emphasized two of her most impressive attributes. Somehow, her blouse had become unbuttoned so that a bit of bare flesh seemed squirming to escape.

"Very stable." The words sounded strained to my own ears. She crossed her legs and her skirt slid back.

"A man with your job, often so far from home, out by yourself, must be tempted. Your restraint speaks well for the bonds with your mate," she said quietly, looking into my eyes.

"Very strong bonds." So why did I feel like a prisoner who had just discovered his cell's door had been left unlocked?

"I think you're a lonely man. You spend your life holding back, keeping your own counsel. That's not good. It's not natural. You need release."

I stared at her. Several seconds ticked by. "Are you sure your body isn't wracked with social diseases?"

As silence grew, she smiled and stepped up to me, slowly welding her pelvis against my aroused instrument, pressing her breasts into my chest. "No herpes." She brushed her lips over my cheek. "No AIDS." She breathed in my ear. "No syphilis." Her mouth found its way to mine. "No clap."

I'm not sure every possible symptom had been checked off. It was too late now. We were kissing, her mouth open and her tongue moving. I put my arms around her to pull her even tighter against me. Minutes later the lights were out and we were in bed, naked, while I buried my face in her breasts that had once stood up firm for the camera. She was writhing under me, begging me to enter her. I thrust into her and she pulled me deeper, deeper still, until neither of us could resist any longer.

The phone rang much later. Arlene was curled up, her back to me, snoring softly, while my hand still lay upon her breasts. The phone rang again. I pulled my right arm from under Arlene's head and swung my legs over the edge of the bed. The luminous dial of my watch showed 1:17.

Grumpily into the phone I said, "Yeah."

"Better get over here right away." It was Hammond's voice. Who else would have known I was there?

"Why should I want to do that?"

"I heard from Gault a little while ago."

"Can't you tell me about it after breakfast?"

"I didn't figure you'd want to wait that long. You see, he was here. And then he left. He took Brandon with him."

14

HAMMOND'S HOUSE WAS the only one in the neighborhood with lights on when I turned onto Glenwood Avenue. Night had not done much to diminish the heat of the day. The air was so humid I had had to run my windshield wipers to clear off the condensed moisture before I set out. I parked once again in Hammond's driveway and started up to the front door. The slam of the car door behind me seemed unnaturally loud in the stillness.

Esther Hammond was waiting in the doorway for me. "Come in." She opened the screen door and stood aside.

Her husband was in the living room wearing a pair of trousers but no shirt. As I stepped across the threshold, he was slamming a magazine into the butt of a .45 Commander.

He jacked a shell into the chamber for dramatic effect for my benefit, put on the safety, and stuck the piece in the waistband of his pants.

"A little late for that, isn't it?" I asked. "Something about closing the barn door after the horse is gone."

"I got lax," Hammond admitted. "It's being retired. For the first time in my life I didn't have a loaded gun in my hand when I answered my door late at night. Worse than that, I let myself underestimate Gault."

"I put a pot of coffee on." Despite the heat, Esther wore a flannel nightgown that went up to her throat. She wore a robe over that, which she held shut with the fingers of one hand. I wondered if she wore a wet suit in the bathtub. "You would appreciate some, no doubt."

"I would."

We adjourned to the kitchen and took seats around the table. Esther poured coffee into a pair of thick mugs and set them before her husband and me.

"What happened?" I asked.

"We were in bed when someone knocked on the door. I got up to answer it, thinking maybe it was you. It was Gault, acting wimpy and upset." Hammond's voice rose half an octave as he mimicked his son-in-law, " 'Something terrible has happened. I have to talk to you,' he said, like he didn't have the faintest idea we had anything to do with Brandon. Hell, I was half asleep and off my guard. I let him in. Soon as he had Esther and me in here, he pulled a gun and got the drop on us."

"What kind of gun?"

"Four-inch Python, my old service revolver that I gave him for an anniversary present after I retired. I also taught him how to use it, if you're wondering. He's a pretty fair shot."

I inhaled some coffee, feeling my vital signs start to register. "Then what?"

"He herded Esther and me down in the basement and locked the door on us." He nodded to a door off the kitchen. It had a simple slide bolt and hasp on this side that had been smashed out of the wall, ripping away part of the frame. "It took me awhile to get us out. By that time he had grabbed Brandon and was gone."

I sipped more coffee and lit a cigarette. Esther got up and rattled through a cupboard until she came up with a cracked saucer, probably the nearest thing the house had to an ashtray. "Got any idea where he went?"

"Where did you take Arlene?"

"Same motel where I'm staying."

A light of understanding flicked in his eyes and he struggled to keep from showing a smile. He understood that I had been tricked as much as he had. "That will be his first stop."

"What makes you think that?"

"Son, I told you Gault was carrying on with another woman before Tricia died. Who do you think the other woman was?"

"Arlene." Maybe the reason I had never asked the question before was that I hadn't wanted my suspicions confirmed.

"Of all the men who have known that hussy's foul body, she had to go after her own sister's husband. Incest." Esther pronounced it as if she were delivering a guilty verdict.

"She came here to make sure we had Brandon. As soon as she knew, she passed the word to Gault," Hammond reasoned.

I thought about his theory. "It won't wash. Arlene never had a chance to contact Gault or let him know where she's staying."

"Then we've got time to run her down there." Hammond

went into another room and came out putting on a golf shirt, letting it hang outside his trousers to conceal his .45. "I'll follow you in my car. Don't try anything if you get ahead of me."

I drove back to the motel feeling as if I were wearing grooves in the road on the route. Hammond stuck with me all the way, driving his Jeep Wagoneer. The parking lot of the motel was quiet when we arrived. I put my car in the same slot as before and waited for Hammond to catch up after he had found a space. I went to my door and took out the key. Through the window, I could see the room was dark, the way I had left it.

"So she's staying with you," Hammond whispered as if he were getting confirmation of what he already knew.

Hammond took up a position on the hinge side of the door and drew his automatic, using a two-hand grip, muzzle down. I unlocked the door, pushed it open, flicked the light switch and stepped into my room, Hammond lagging behind. Arlene was not in the bed or the bathroom and her overnight bag was gone.

"She lit out," Hammond surmised, "on her way to meet Gault. He must have been watching the house while Arlene was there. She gave him some kind of sign when she left with you. Might have been the way she carried her bag—over her left shoulder if Brandon was there, over her right if he wasn't. Something like that. Then she went off with you to make sure you didn't leave your room until Gault had done his dirty work. After I called you and you left, she went to Gault."

Painful as the admission was, I agreed. I sat down on the foot of my unmade bed and began untying my shoelaces.

"What are you doing?" Hammond asked.

"Going back to sleep."

"What good will that do?"

"What good will it do to stay up all night?" I countered. "This way I'll at least be halfway fresh in the morning. There's nothing more we can do tonight."

"Still going to Cincy in the morning?"

Hammond had slipped into a habit of thought that made us partners, two ex-cops searching for the same man. We had that in common, and I could see that cooperating might be more helpful than fighting him. "I guess so. Gault might have gone there or he might have gone back to Cleveland. If not one of those two places, anywhere else in the world. At least if I go to Cincinnati, I can dig into background I haven't covered before."

"Then I'll head for Cleveland in case he returns home. That way we cover twice the territory. See you there in a couple days?"

We agreed that Hammond would leave word at my office where he could be reached, and he left. Still in my shirt and pants, I turned out the lights and stretched out on my bed, telling myself I would not fall asleep. Even so I nearly dozed off and shocked myself into sitting up. Fifteen minutes had passed since Hammond had left. I put on my shoes and went outside. No sign of Hammond or his Wagoneer. I went down to the office of the motel. At this time of night the lobby was closed, but a room full of vending machines was open, with a window into the desk where the sleepy-eyed clerk was poring over a college accounting text.

I wrenched him away from his studies and asked for a record of the calls made from my room. He punched some keys on his computer and got a printout with one call, a toll charge, made at 1:32 AM, minutes after I had left for Hammond's. The clerk recognized the prefix as a Decatur exchange.

"Anything wrong?" he asked.

I told him I didn't think so. "Has a woman been here tonight since, say 1:30? Late thirties, stacked, dark hair, and a blue dress?"

"Sure was. If I hadn't noticed her, I'd be ready for a white cane and a tin cup."

"What was she doing here?"

"Waiting, I guess. First I saw her, she was just outside the office, pacing up and down, smoking a cigarette. Then she came in and got a can of Diet Pepsi. She stood outside and drank it, smoked another cigarette. I tell you, the office is supposed to be closed after midnight, but I was ready to make an exception for her. Then a car came by, she got in, and it drove off."

"What kind of car?"

"Little foreign job."

"Fiat?"

"Could have been."

"How long was she waiting?"

"Half hour, maybe."

"Can you drive here from Decatur in a half hour?"

He thought that would be about right. On a hunch, I turned to the Yellow Pages to the page for "Hotels-Motels" and searched for one with a number that matched the toll call from my room. County Line Motel, Route 33, Decatur.

I returned to my car and pulled out of the motel, running the windshield wipers again, heading for Lafayette Street, which carried me through the deserted business district and became U.S. 33 southeast at the city limits. Not an Interstate but still divided, it moved traffic along at this time of night when all the businesses gauntleting it were closed. I came to a sign maybe fifteen miles from Fort Wayne: Leave Allen County. Enter Adams County. Fifty yards later, I reached the County Line Motel. It was large enough to have a night clerk on duty, and I was prepared to swear the same one from my motel had slipped out the back door and dashed down here ahead of me. This one was reading a text on business management. I asked him for Alan Gault's room.

He reached for his records and stopped with his hand over the registration cards. "Gault? Oh, yeah. He's the one who checked out awhile ago."

"How long ago?"

He pulled the card to be sure. "Hour and a half, at 1:45."

"When did he check in?"

"Four-ten Thursday afternoon, with his wife. I didn't see her when he checked out. She was probably in the car."

"Any children?"

"Just the couple. You have a reason for asking these questions?"

"I'm a shamus." I slapped a twenty on the counter. "Rent me Gault's old room."

"I can't do that. The maid won't even make it up until later this morning."

"I'm not particular."

Uncertain about what he was doing, he slid a key across the desk. Room 23. I picked it up and headed for the door.

"Don't you want to register?" the clerk called after me.

"I'd only use a false name anyway." I drove my car down the line to 23 and entered it. Another undistinguished motel room. The spread was still on the bed but an impression showed someone had rested there. Bathroom towels were all in place with one exception, a small hand towel that had been used. One glass unwrapped. The wastebasket held nothing but wrappers from McDonald's.

I lit a cigarette and sat down in my third motel room of the past two days, the most barren of them all. The whole room was like the bed, undisturbed, with only the slightest impression of human occupancy. In at 4:00 PM and out before 2:00 AM. Gault might never have carried his bags in from the car. I ran over the sequence of events I knew, puttying the cracks with supposition.

Gault had driven Arlene here from Cleveland, arriving in late afternoon, and checked in with her to establish a base of operations, a place to receive phone calls. Close to Fort Wayne but well outside its borders, to prevent any possibility Arlene would be recognized, I guessed. They had eaten a take-out dinner to avoid being seen together in public. Later, when Brandon was sure to be home if there at all, Gault had driven Arlene to downtown Fort Wayne, where she got a taxi to her parents' house, as if she were coming in from the airport. Meanwhile, Gault had gone ahead to find a place to conceal himself with a view of the front door. He saw Arlene go in, saw Hammond and me arrive moments later, saw Arlene leave with me. Hammond's idea of how Arlene might have signaled him was as good a guess as any.

A fleeting thought tickled me. A man who planned this well could scheme to murder his wife.

What would Gault have thought when he saw Arlene leave with me? He wouldn't have dared to follow for fear Hammond and his wife would take Brandon away. Gault had to depend on Arlene getting out by herself. He stayed and watched the house, and when the time came he took Brandon. They drove back to the County Line Motel and waited by the phone.

Meanwhile, Hammond was calling me. How much had I told Arlene as I pulled on my clothes? Half-awake, I had not been very communicative. I hadn't known much to communicate. Stay here, I'll fill you in when I get back. It didn't matter how little I had said. It was enough to clue Arlene that Gault had been successful. As soon as I had gone, she called Gault. Come get me. She dressed and went to wait for him by the office.

When Arlene's call came, Gault had taken Brandon out to his car. He checked out of the motel, picked up Arlene, and drove off to—

It would have been helpful if Gault had left an itinerary for me to find, but he hadn't been that careless. He expected to drive through the night to get there. Surely he didn't expect to drive all day as well. Therefore, he had a destination in mind—at least a stopping point—he could be expected to reach by dawn. This motel, which would have been their jumping-off point according to their original plan, was southeast of Fort Wayne. My mental compass turned southeast in search of a meaningful point that could be reached by dawn. The only thing that came to me that way was Cincinnati.

I returned the Room 23 key to the befuddled night clerk before I drove back into Fort Wayne to my motel, sipping the last of the coffee in my travel mug on the way. It was four o'clock before I entered my room. I set my travel alarm for seven and logged three solid hours of sleep before it went off.

15

FRIDAY MORNING FOUND ME on the road before eight o'clock, heading east on U.S. 30. I crossed the Indiana border back into Ohio a half hour later and stopped for an egg sandwich at the Van Wert Interchange. Munching the sandwich, sipping coffee, I pressed on until I connected with Interstate 75. The mile post marker was 134, telling me how far it was to Cincinnati. Southbound on I-75, I passed Lima and then the Air and Space Museum at Neil Armstrong's home town of Wapakoneta. At Sidney I stopped again for coffee.

Eleven o'clock Ohio time brought me to Dayton. I pulled off there to find a pay phone where I could place a credit-card call to the Cincinnati Police Department, asking for

Sergeant Gilmore in Homicide. He was on duty but out of the office on an investigation, due back by four o'clock. No problem. Mile post markers were now in the fifties. I left my name and promised to check in by one o'clock.

The rest of the trip was an easy coast down I-75. When I reached Cincinnati, I followed the freeway to the downtown exit near Riverfront Stadium and then drove past Fountain Square for sightseeing. Downtown Cincinnati looks like a space station with concrete walkways connecting major buildings at the second-floor level. You can go from hotel to department store to theater without touching ground. The first time I ever saw it, it had turned me off. I thought it related to a real downtown the way Riverfront Stadium relates to a real ball park. Then, like Riverfront, it grows on you. Someday Hollywood will discover it as a great place to stage a running gun battle.

North of Fountain Square I worked my way over to Ezzard Charles Drive leading up to the empty shell of what used to be Union Station. Police headquarters lies off the driveway leading up to the terminal, built by an architect who began designing junior high schools in the suburbs. I found a parking space and went inside where, like any big city police station, policemen wander around aimlessly, showing no concern for crime outside their fortress. When I stated my business, they gave me a visitor's tag and escorted me to the Homicide office where the desk with the name plate *Sgt. Darius Gilmore* was empty.

"He's on his way in," my escort assured me. "There was a stabbing on Fourth Street. It's all settled now."

I sat down to wait at Gilmore's desk. Across the room, two detectives were talking to a thin black youth who must have been on the scene of the stabbing. They were trying to get him to admit he had seen it go down.

"I didn't see nothin', man . . . I don't know the dudes, man. Never saw them before . . . Man, I wasn't lookin' that way . . . I be lookin' at the store across the street . . . No, man, it ain't got no windows to reflect nothin' . . . They boarded up."

The detectives kept at him for a good five minutes trying to trip him on something.

"Did you at least see the dude in the yellow T-shirt," one asked at last.

"They wasn't no dude in a yellow T-shirt."

"Benny, how can you say he *wasn't* there unless you saw what happened?"

"I didn't see nothin', man."

One of the detectives gave up in exasperation. "Benny, I can't help you. You don't need a cop. You need an eye doctor."

For me, listening to all that was as painful as seeing the girl who jilted you out on a date with another guy. While I was thinking that, Gilmore arrived stripping off his sports coat. "You're the P.I. waiting to see me? Disbro?"

"That's right." I stood up and shook hands with him. We satisfied each other we had been working out with the squeezers. Gilmore was half a head shorter than I am, with the skin texture of a bowling ball. He was broad and thick so that when he sat down, he didn't look much different than he had standing up. "What brings you all the way from Cleveland?"

"A year ago March you had a suicide case, a woman named Patricia Gault."

"Again?" Gilmore asked in surprise. "It was only last week another rent-a-cop came through here about the same thing."

"Really? What did you tell him?"

"The coroner calls it suicide, it stays suicide. Christ Almighty, we've got enough to do here without going out of our way to bring in business. What's your angle on this anyway? Insurance?"

"Employment check," I lied glibly. "Professor Gault is applying for a job in private industry, and we're looking into his background. I understand there was some question about his wife's death."

"You must have been talking to his in-laws. They won't believe their daughter killed herself no matter what."

"I suppose that's where it originated."

Gilmore rubbed his palm over his jaw line. "You been to the prosecutor to get permission to inspect the files?"

"Not yet. I came straight here to find out what the procedure should be."

"You should go to the prosecutor." Gilmore rocked his swivel chair. "That's what the guy last week did." He rocked some more. "Of course, that would take you the rest of the afternoon, meaning you couldn't start until tomorrow, when I'm going to be tied up testifying in court." He reached a conclusion. "Hell, I don't see why I can't let you have a peek and settle it today. Usually a file this old would be in the Records Room, but I think it's still here from the other guy."

Gilmore got up and went to a file cabinet near the desk where the detectives were still trying to restore Benny's eyesight. "How many times I gotta tell you, man? I saw nothin'." Gilmore searched through the files and pulled out a thick folder. He looked inside it to make sure it was the right one, closed the drawer and turned around, standing behind Benny's shoulder.

"Tell you what, Benny," Gilmore offered. "You tell these men what they need to know and it stays here. Keep lying to us and I go back to the neighborhood and start spreading the word you snitched."

"Hey, man! That's not fair!"

"Who said I was fair?" Gilmore came back to his desk and sat down, plopping the folder on his blotter. He drew a stack of eight-by-ten color photos from the file and tapped their edges even as if he were getting ready to deal a deck of cards. "How's your stomach?"

"The first suicide I ever rolled on was a case where the guy swallowed the barrel of his shotgun. It's been downhill ever since."

Gilmore handed me the photos. "Where were you a cop?"

"Cleveland. I still am, technically. I'm on layoff subject to recall when finances permit, which isn't going to happen." I picked up the photos and looked the situation over. The top photo was a medium long shot of the body in the basement. A clothesline rope had been tied around a pipe between rafters in the ceiling, leaving room for the noose. The knot was a loop in the end of the rope with the opposite end thrust through it like a cowboy's lasso. Tricia's head was inside the noose, the knot under her left ear, her hair grazing the rafters.

The basement ceiling had been too low to allow her to swing free. Her heels were on the cement floor, her body half-folded into an L shape.

"It means nothing that the body doesn't swing free," Gilmore lectured me. "We see suicides in the damnedest positions. Had a guy once who hanged himself off the foot of the bed, sitting with his ass an inch off the floor. Prisoners that hang themselves in their cell usually manage it by tying their blanket to the cell door and going down on their knees. The important thing is to put enough pressure on the neck to cut off circulation. Do that and the job is done."

"I know." The other photos were close-ups of aspects in the first one—Tricia's jogging shoes on their heels, the clothesline tied to the pipe, the knot behind Tricia's ear, Tricia's face with her tongue filling her open mouth, the clothesline biting into the flesh of her throat. She had been wearing stretch pants and a short-sleeve sweater over her blouse, eye shadow, lipstick and rouge. "How long was she hanging before she was found?"

"Two hours max."

I put the photos back on his desk. Gilmore had packed a pipe and was squirting flame into its bowl from a butane lighter. "Her face is white," I commented.

"She was white all over. Not everyone is blessed with skin color as lovely as mine."

"The knot was on the side of her neck. That turns the face red. A white face in a strangulation case means the knot should be at the back."

"Nothing pisses me off like a cop who reads the manual." Gilmore took the pipe out of his teeth and looked in the bowl to make sure it was burning evenly. "The coroner considered that point. He figured the body might have rotated inside the noose when people started coming in the house, stamping feet, slamming doors and such. More important is the condition of her neck where the rope bites into it." He selected the close-up of her throat and showed it to me again, pointing out the significant features with his pipestem. "See those bruise marks around the rope just below it here and here? There's one above it. Means she was alive when the rope bit into her throat."

"But not that she was hanging there."

"Let me anticipate where you're headed," Gilmore said, leaning back in his chair, puffing his pipe. "You want to say Gault came up behind her and strangled her with a length of this same rope, tying a knot at back. Later, he strung her up in the basement so that the noose fit in the same grooves. It won't wash. If she was garroted from behind—like taking out a sentry in wartime—the rope marks would be nearly horizontal, whereas a noose makes marks going upward toward the rear at a severe angle. In other words, for your theory to work, there would have to be two sets of marks. There was only one and she was in the noose when she died. Sorry."

"Nothing to be sorry about," I told him. "I'm only checking out the possibilities. If this is a righteous suicide, so be it."

"It is, but let's say you still want to build a case against Gault. Start with the fact she died in the noose. That's the one thing you can't get around. So how would he get her into the noose? 'Here, dear, stick your head in there. Now sort of sag down. Trust me.'" Gilmore shook his head. "I know what my wife would say if I tried something like that. So what else do you have? He drugged her first? No drugs in her body. Hit her over the head? No marks of violence. Simply overpowered her and forced her head into the noose? While she's kicking and screaming? Again, no marks on her and just as significant, no marks on him."

Gilmore relit his pipe, which had gone out. "Against all that, you have a couple outside facts to support suicide. One, she dolled herself up with makeup and all, even though she was only home doing the laundry, which is typical of female suicides. Two, she left a note."

"She did?" It was the first time I had heard of it.

Gilmore reached into the file again and produced a small stack of handwritten papers. They were steno-sized sheets of stationery with Patricia Gault's name and address printed at the top on off-white paper. The writing was done in purple ink, roundly feminine with circles for dots over the *i*'s, and *t*'s crossed with a wavy line. "Before you ask, handwriting analysis established it was hers without a doubt."

I read through the five sides in a hurry. "Any chance I could get a copy of this?"

"Didn't you ever hear of Xerox? I'll run you off some before you leave."

I lit a cigarette and studied Gilmore's face. "Did you turn anything on the way Gault was playing around?"

"Sure. He was dipping his wick in his own sister-in-law, who once posed nude in a girlie mag. What of it? Every man needs a hobby. According to that suicide note, his wife wasn't guiltless. After all they were both intellectual college types who believe in free love and open marriages. Assume that Tricia found out about the affair and killed herself over it. That still don't make Gault guilty of murder, not in the eyes of the law at least."

"I guess not." I flicked ashes into the tray on his desk.

"Maybe I've got a treat for you." He went through his desk drawers until he found what he was looking for, a slick paper page with printed columns on one side and a photo on the other. "One of the men found this in a back issue of a magazine. It didn't properly belong with the case file. On the other hand, I couldn't see throwing it away."

I unfolded the photo and saw Arlene posed in a reclining position, pouting petulantly at the camera, her breasts thrust forward, nipples erect, one hand casually covering her muff. "Nothing I haven't seen before." The comment probably had more significance for me than Gilmore.

"Let me get your copy of the letter." He went off to find a copy machine, leaving me alone with the folder on his desk. It might not have been deliberate, but I picked it up anyway.

The report was amazingly complete. It had floor plans of the Gault house, including the basement with the laundry room adjacent to the room where Tricia had hung. There were photos of the rooms, one showing a basket of laundry beside the washing machine, a few items of clothes hanging out the door. Tricia had started to do a wash but changed her mind and decided to kill herself instead.

The narrative report of the investigation was just as complete. For a man with little time to spare from stabbings and shootings, Gilmore had put a lot of time on this suicide. He had questioned people at the university about Gault's alibi and Mr. and Mrs. Pankow, who lived next door. They had apparently known about the affair with Arlene and given him other names to check, most of them involved with the local TV stations. Gault had once gone to a historical society meeting in Denver and checked into the hotel with his wife. But on the same day Tricia had been in Cincinnati hosting a group of faculty wives who were raising money for children in Ethiopia.

For all the effort Gilmore had put into it, nothing had changed the facts of the case. They stayed the way we had discussed them, a suicide.

"Finding everything you need?" Gilmore asked as he walked into the office and handed me the photocopies of the suicide note.

"Nice work." I closed the file folder and put it back on his desk.

"Paperwork is a bitch but damned if it doesn't come in handy every so often."

I took out Monk John's marked map of Cincinnati and showed it to him. "This map was willed to me. All those marks are supposed to be significant of something to do with this case. Can you make them out?"

Puffing his pipe, Gilmore studied the map. He took his pipe out of his teeth and again used the stem as a pointer. "Police headquarters." He moved the stem up to the university area. "Gault's house." The stem traveled west to

Colerain. "The nude model's condo." East to Indian Hill. "Don't know." Southwest across the river to Newport on the Kentucky side. "Don't know." Those last two had left him frowning.

"Maybe I'll figure it out later." I folded the map and put it away, then copied down the exact addresses from the report.

"Anything else I can do for you?"

"Start signing your paychecks over to me? That's about the only thing you haven't done so far."

If it was possible for Gilmore to blush, he did it then. "Us cops gotta stick together. Nobody else is going to do it for us."

We shook hands again, another muscle draw, and parted on that note. I wanted to get away from the police department and find someplace where I could read the suicide note again. I wanted to make sure it said what I thought because of another idea gnawing at me.

I had seen a way that Tricia's death could have been a murder after all.

16

WHILE I WAS DOWNTOWN, I decided to treat myself to a full lunch on the expense account. I found a parking lot on Walnut and went to Ted Kluszewski's Place. It was the end of the lunch rush, so I had no trouble getting a table. When I had put in my order, I moseyed into the bar and examined some of Ted's memorabilia on display. One of the items on the wall was an old magazine cover showing Ted with Gus Bell, whose son Buddy is now playing for the Reds.

I went back to my table in time to receive my meal. Food in my stomach only combined with my lack of sleep to make me drowsy. I lingered over extra coffee as long as I dared and decided to try walking it off. It was only a short stroll from Ted's restaurant to Fountain Square under a hazy sky that made the sidewalk radiate heat through the soles of my shoes. Even the tropical tan suit I was wearing was too much for the weather—except that a third of the men I saw were wearing one just like mine. People down here had adapted to heat like Southerners. That thought led me to consider the places I had been those past two days.

Cincinnati, as close to Nashville as to Cleveland, could claim to be the most northern of all Southern cities in its accents and pace of life. Literally south of the Mason–Dixon line, farther south than Baltimore, separated by only the Ohio River from Kentucky, born on the banks of a paddle-wheel culture that led directly to New Orleans, Cincinnati could hardly have turned out otherwise. And thus my travels, barely out of a two hundred–mile radius of Cleveland, had taken me through the convergence of three major areas of the country.

I found a shady spot to sit on the steps above the fountains, where I took out the note Tricia had written and examined it in detail:

Dearest Alan,

What I am about to do may shock you and confound you, although it shouldn't after all the years we have been together. It is a natural outgrowth of all that has gone before. You could probably tell me that someone once said, "Our past is but the prelude to the future." I was never any good at footnoting quotations, as you so well know. I always depended on you for that kind of thing, as I have depended on you in the past for so much. Anyway, the quotation is not important; its thought is. What I am today is simply the sum total of all my yesterdays. Alan, the clues are all there if only you would look for them. I am not suddenly going off the track. I am following a course that was mapped out for me the day I was born. You won't call it God's Will—but my folks would. In my heart, I suppose I would, too. So you call it fate or determinism or any other academic word you wish.

You see, dear, to a large extent my marriage to you has been a denial of that Divine Will, a denial of my very nature. You know what I was when we met—a dewy-eyed maiden from the Corn Belt. You always knew what culture shock I faced when I arrived at college. Sodom U. and College of Gomorrah, I thought. How I prayed not to succumb to the temptations of Sex and Drugs and Free Thinking. All that Puritanical upbringing was challenged every moment I was in class. (Possible exception: math.) Science contradicted Creationism. Literature suggested that the Bible had not been dictated by God and some of the books were not written by the men credited with them. History put the stories of Exodus or Chronicles in a larger context. That was the point in my life when I was facing a crisis of faith.

Enter Instructor Alan Gault. Remember all those discussions we had after class? You solved my crisis of faith in the strangest way—not by giving me answers but by teaching me there is no such thing as Received Wisdom. There is no authority to tell me how to think about what subjects. You taught me these were things I had to work out for myself.

What a horrible thing to do to a woman like me!

Why did you spend so much time on me? Was it all an indirect seduction? Was it a form of hubris in your abilities as a teacher? Did you see yourself as Rex Harrison remolding Pygmalion? At the time I thought you were my deliverer. I thought you had opened new vistas on which we could base our life together. We tried, but it was all a false premise. I was not being freed; I was being sentenced. There is an element of the jailer in every teacher. In order to impart knowledge, you have to herd your students into a classroom and shut the door. That is how it worked out for me. I closed a door on my past when we married and locked a part of myself away.

The years that followed were better to you than to me. Your career plodded along. I tried to play the good faculty wife. I gave you a son. It was all so different from anything I had known before, so different that I have never really adapted to it. You recognized that yourself, even if you would never own up to it. Proof? Your affair with Arlene is proof that you were searching for something away from home. Surprised that I know? After all the pains you took to be discreet? Didn't it ever occur to you that I could be just as discreet when I turned to an affair outside marriage? Who was it who liberated me to consider the unthinkable?

Now comes today and my Ultimate Act of Defiance. You will puzzle over it and even feel guilt, which you shouldn't. You will try to explain why I have done something so uncharacteristic, and that will be your mistake. My Ultimate Act of Defiance is no aberration. It is a natural consequence. Ask Cora, who may or may not discuss it with you. I have sworn her to a vow of silence, though she may feel released after today.

Above all, Alan, do not blame yourself. You cannot help being what you are any more than I can help being what I am. If any mistake was made, it was a joint one when we both conspired to try altering the direction of my life. You could not have done it without my consent. If anything, that means the major portion of any blame rests with me.

Give my love to Brandon and remember me always as

Your loving wife,
Tricia

After reading it through for the third time, I put the photocopies away in my inside coat pocket and walked back to the lot to redeem my car. Cora? The name was not one that had ever come up before. Yet she was obviously someone Tricia had confided in, someone who might have been able to steer me to the man with whom Tricia had been unfaithful. These concerns were on my mind as I drove up Vine Street into the hills that rose from the riverfront.

The University of Cincinnati sits on a hill from which it can look down on the proletariat below, sniffing a more rarefied air of academic freedom and pure knowledge. The address for the Gaults had been inside the triangle formed by Ludlow, Clifton, and McAlpin, a kind of Faculty Row of well-preserved homes on winding streets untouched by the urban blight creeping up from below. Their house was a sturdy Georgian brick, now in the hands of another family. Next door in a similar home was the Pankow residence that had supplied so much of Gilmore's information. It was empty with a realtor's sign in the yard.

I turned around and came back to park in the shade of an elm. Out of luck. The new owners of the Gault house would probably know nothing beyond the rumors that their home was haunted. The Pankows had moved on. While I sat drumming my fingers on the steering wheel, the door of the house across the street opened and a woman came out dressed in old clothes and a Chinese coolie hat, holding a hand hoe. She went to the rose bushes bordering her front walk and began digging out weeds around them. She might be worth a try. I got out of my car and walked up to her.

"Excuse me."

She looked up, mildly startled, quickly smiling a greeting. "May I help you, young man?"

"Maybe I'm confused in my directions. Doesn't Professor Gault live around here?"

"He used to." She stood up with surprising agility for someone who must have been well beyond sixty. She gestured with her hand hoe. "That was his home until last year. He sold it to another faculty member and moved away entirely. Not that you can blame him, after the tragedy. Do you know about that?"

"His wife died, didn't she?"

"Killed herself, that's what. It wasn't a surprise to anyone around here except the professor himself. Anyone could have told you Tricia was on a self-destructive course."

For once I had lucked out. This woman was willing to talk with only a minimum of prompting. "I never detected that but I barely met her."

"She could be that way, able to put on a front for a short time. You didn't have to be around her long to see through it. I never saw anyone so inadequate for the life she had chosen. She should have married a shoe store clerk and never had another thought the rest of her life. Why he married her, I'll never know. She was nothing but a millstone around his neck. Of course, men of genius sometimes marry women with whom they have nothing in common. Beethoven, for instance. There should be an interesting paper in that proposition if you would care to pursue it."

I felt I had been given an assignment. "Exactly how was Tricia so inadequate?"

"She wasn't stupid, exactly. She had a bachelor's degree and had taught school. For all that, she was—stunted. It was her fundamentalist background as near as I can detect. It had set limits to her life that she never dared to cross. When she married, she gave up her career and her imagination as a package deal. Honestly, what could she have discussed with her husband? Alan was dealing with research into the problems of mankind and Tricia was watching Ernest Angley on the tube."

I turned away from her and looked at the house next door, with the real estate sign in the yard. "Isn't that where the Pankows lived?"

"Yes, they moved out, too." She breathed regret. "This neighborhood is changing. Soon only my rose bushes will remain."

"Weren't they rather friendly with the Gaults?"

"More so than anyone else around."

"Is that why they moved? Because they couldn't stand living next to the house where Tricia died?"

"Nothing that dramatic. He was promoted so they decided they could afford something better. They moved to Indian Hill. He had been some kind of accountant in the bursar's office. Then he was promoted to a position in charge of the computer that does all the student scheduling."

"You wouldn't have their current address?"

"I could find it easily enough if you will wait a moment."

I waited while she went into the house, thinking about her remarks about marriage. I have seen some strange match-ups in my time without worrying overmuch about what a couple can find in one another. By the standards of compatibility, Linda and I should have been an ideal couple—she a reporter, me a cop—but our marriage had been like three falls of Big Time Wrestling. It might have been easier for her if the radio station had renewed her contract, but her bosses had claimed she had a conflict of interest covering the police beat when her husband was on the force. She probably felt she had given up too much when she married me and resented me for it. She proved she was probably right, because a month after she moved out, she landed a producing job with the TV station. Then I was laid off and met Helen.

There was another odd coupling. It was plain enough what I saw in Helen—beauty, intelligence, vivaciousness, curiosity. What could I possibly contribute to the brew? Maybe it was what I had suggested back in Cleveland, that we were teaching each other new ways of thinking. I was still thinking about that when the woman returned with an address book in her hand.

"Here it is." She read off the address to me as I jotted it down in my notebook.

"How do you spell that street?" I asked.

She turned the address book so I could see for myself. Their names were Edward and Cora Pankow.

17

THE FREEWAY SYSTEM CARRIED ME across the north side of Cincinnati toward the suburb of Indian Hill. On a Friday afternoon, outbound traffic was already beginning to thicken as the toilers slipped out early to get a head start on the weekend. At a service station at Miami and Camargo, I paused to pump gas into my tank and study Monk's map. The address for Edward and Cora Pankow was inside the circle he had drawn in Indian Hill.

It was a street still under development. The old end, nearest the main drag, might have been three years old and lined with houses you wouldn't want to think about without a lot of money in your kitty. The street was dirtied by chunks of mud that had clunked off the tractor treads of construction machinery. Farther down the street, the last completed house gave way to homes still under construction and sided by silver Celotex. Beyond them were a few skeleton frames and beyond the frames, staked-out lots. Farther still, bulldozers were clearing trees.

Pankow's house was third from the end of the completed homes, California influences showing in its Spanish design and red tile roof. The front door was recessed in a tiny patio with a locked iron gate across its front. Three rings of the doorbell got me nowhere. I would have given up at that point except I could hear loud music coming from the side of the house—loud enough to drown out the sound of the doorbell. I homed in on the sound like a heat-seeking missile. It drew me around the side of the house toward the back yard, which was surrounded by a brick wall that had a gate between the house and the garage. The gate had a simple latch that I unhooked and went through.

A swimming pool lay beyond the gate. Beside the pool was the ghetto blaster that was producing the music. Next to the radio was an air mattress. On the air mattress reclined a young woman applying sun screen to her flesh. I hoped the sun screen had a high protection factor because it was all she had to fend off the rays. Maybe a gentleman under those circumstances would have closed his eyes and withdrawn. For whatever it makes me, I stood where I was and looked. The girl was a teenager, her hair style and makeup showing she was a Madonna fan. Her body was slim, almost boyish, with small breasts like a pair of eggs sunny-side up. As she applied sun tan lotion to the back of her shoulder, her eyes strayed my way and then picked me up. For the longest time nothing happened. I gave her a two-finger salute. She screwed the top back on the bottle of lotion, wiped her hands on a towel, and reached out to shut off the radio. The contrast between the noise and the sudden silence convinced me I had suddenly gone stone deaf. "Cora!" the girl called. "Company!"

It occurred to me there were other objects back here I could be looking at. One of them was a chaise longue positioned with its back to me. The top of a head appeared over the back, rising until a pair of eyes covered by wraparound sunglasses could see. The head went down, arms flailed, and she stood up from the chaise pulling a robe around her. Until the robe, the sunglasses had been her entire ensemble. Cora tied the belt of her robe, stepped into a pair of clogs, and advanced along the apron of the swimming pool toward me, clopping a determined rhythm.

"What do you want?" she demanded.

"I want to dig up your past." I showed her my identification. "The subject is Tricia Gault."

"My God, do you people operate in tandem?" Cora Pankow was short and hefty with a physique that could have given Rowdy Roddy Piper trouble in two falls out of three. Below her sunglasses, her thin mouth was drawn taut. Above, her hair was done in one of those defiantly unattractive hairdos—tight on one side, loose on the other.

"Has someone else been here?"

"Another private detective, from Indianapolis. All my life I never knew there were such things. Now they start showing up one every other week. At least you're fairly presentable."

"John Monk was his name?"

She nodded. "He looked more like one of the Smith Brothers."

"Did you answer his questions?"

"Except the ones that were too personal."

"Then you shouldn't have any trouble answering mine."

Cora turned to the young woman on the air mattress. "Better go inside, Melissa."

The girl pouted. "I just got ready for a tan. You like me to be tanned. You always say that."

"You won't have to stay inside very long. We won't need much time to discuss our business."

Melissa stood up and Cora put an arm around her shoulders, walking her toward the sliding glass patio doors. As they went, Melissa kept bumping her hip into Cora's, and Cora let her arm slide down Melissa's back toward her butt while she whispered into Melissa's ear. Halfway to the doors, they stopped and Cora kissed her. Their age difference was right, but I didn't think Cora was her mother. Melissa went on and Cora came back to me.

"Why all this interest in Tricia of late?" she asked.

"The circumstances of her death are a question mark. Now that her husband is being considered for a job, his employers want to see what's there."

"So they send two detectives?"

"Maybe he applied at two different places," I lied quickly. "There seems to be some speculation that he drove her to suicide."

"The way Charles Boyer tried to drive Ingrid Bergman nuts in that old flick? Nothing so melodramatic." Cora gestured toward an umbrella-shaded table. "Let's sit over there. I have to watch my skin this late in life."

We meandered that way and Cora answered the question. "Alan Gault is what he's always been, your typical academic, a man lost in his studies and his teaching. Tricia came from an entirely different world, one that was in many ways opposed to Alan's life-style. She attempted to fit in but she couldn't make the adjustment. She killed herself out of frustration."

We had reached the table. I held a chair for her and then went around to the other side where I could sit facing her. "Tricia confided all this in you?"

"I suppose I was her closest friend. My husband is part of the university community but not involved in the academic side. And we lived side by side, so it was natural for us to drop in on each other for coffee and such."

"That's why Tricia told her husband to ask you for an explanation."

"She did? How?"

"In her suicide note."

"I never knew she left one."

I took out the photocopy and showed it to her. Cora scanned the pages and then excused herself to go to her purse by the chaise where she exchanged her sunglasses for a pair of reading half glasses. Ready now, she sat in her chair and read the note through. Drawing on a cigarette, I watched her face change from mild curiosity through degrees of sorrow to anguish. When she was done she handed the note back to me and went to a box of Kleenex. "Damn that allergy," she said coming back.

"Gault never talked to you about any of this?"

She shook her head and blew her nose again. That done, she looked at me over her glasses with eyes the color of bread crust. It was my first sight of them. "Maybe he didn't have to. Maybe he didn't want to find out."

My eyes shuttled toward the house, where Melissa had gone. "That wasn't your daughter."

"A friend," Cora told me.

I folded the photocopy pages carefully and put them back in my inside coat pocket.

"Do you want me to say it?" she asked bluntly. "I'm not ashamed. I'm a dyke."

Hardly a surprising admission. "When Tricia mentions having an affair—" I left a blank for her to fill in.

"We had one." Cora rubbed the palms of her hands against one another as if she were disposing of the detritus of an ancient episode. "I don't hear you gasping in shocked surprise."

"It's a little late in the twentieth century for that."

"For some people it's still mid-Victorian times, believe me. I've seen reactions more appropriate to the seventeenth century and witch trials."

"I'm more surprised that Tricia would be involved."

"Let me have one of your cigarettes." When I had given her one and lit it for her, Cora looked at it and said, "I'm supposed to have quit." She inhaled another puff. "You wouldn't be so surprised if you had really known Tricia. All that preaching she heard throughout her life about the evils of sex, about how lustful men are, about the degradation of women—it all had to have an effect on her. In a way, it's too bad she wasn't a Catholic. Then she could have become a nun, maybe in one of the orders that service the church. I really think she could have been happy there. Since she wasn't Catholic, since she wasn't working out in marriage, what was left for her?"

"You," I suggested.

Cora inhaled my Camel. "Let's get something straight. I'm not into gay liberation. I don't parade for lesbian rights. I don't proselytize. I do my thing on my own reservation and I tell the world to get bent. Clear enough? So when Tricia started unloading on me, I was there only to listen. We got to know each other better, she started crying on my shoulder, one thing led to another—and it happened. I don't suppose you would understand that?"

"Once," I said almost wistfully, "there was a woman who

had just been through a bad emotional scene. I invited her up to my place to dry her tears and talk. Then we had a couple drinks. The next thing I knew, we were in bed."

"There you are, just the way it happened with us. After it was over Tricia was hit by a downpour of guilt. 'My God, what have I done!' That sort of thing. I lectured her about the four sexes..I tried to put it in the historical context. Would you believe I even went over Paul's epistles to put his statements in the context of his time? We had coffee and talk again the next couple days and thrashed it out every way. About a week later—it seemed like a decade—she came to me again. After that, the affair was on."

Cora crushed out her cigarette in a glass ashtray on the table. "It lasted three good months as Tricia's guilt faded and we had opportunities to while away an afternoon."

"What ended it? Did your husband catch you?"

"Edward?" She managed a small laugh. "Excuse me, but I just had a small vision of what that scene would have been like. He would have excused himself for interrupting and then backed out and gone to hacking on his computer. Edward's concept of carnal knowledge is what goes on between a man and a microchip. We long ago reached an accommodation on our marriage. I'm vaguely aware of his flings with college boys in computer science and he's vaguely aware of my activities, and all the while we maintain the outward appearance of a married couple for cover. No, Edward never discovered Tricia and me. I think the novelty simply wore off for Tricia. She felt it was time to move on to other relationships."

"How did that happen?"

The sound of an automobile pulling into the driveway interrupted Cora's narration. Another sound, a garage door rising on a Genie motor, followed. Soon the garage door went down again and a side walk-in door leading into the patio opened. The man who came through it was tall and thin with five strands of hair across his balding skull like the lines of a G clef. He wore a pink shirt with a pale blue suit, a clip-on bow tie and Hush Puppies and carried a copy of *Byte* thick enough to be the phone book of a small city.

"Home already, Edward?" Cora asked.

"No point in staying longer. I finished all I could accomplish for today until that damned English department comes up with their autumn schedule. Why are they the ones always so slow to decide who will handle those freshman composition courses? Every last entering freshman has to take those useless classes, so my whole programming business is held up until—" He broke off when he noticed me. "Hello."

"This is Gilbert Disbro, a private investigator from Cleveland," Cora said to explain my presence.

"Really? Another one?"

I stood up to shake hands with him. Pankow had the pallor of a man who gets his rays from a CRT and the thick glasses to confirm every worst fear about time spent in front of a video screen. "Your wife was just about to tell me about a special friend of Tricia Gault's."

"Deirdre, I suppose you mean. Quite an artist in her own right. Cora could talk about her for hours. Don't let me disturb you." Pankow went over to the chaise and settled in to read *Byte*.

"Deirdre Leminaux," Cora expanded, spelling the name for me. "She was a sometime student of modern art who opened a small shop to sell art supplies on Vine Street just off the campus. I introduced her to Tricia when she was canvassing her friends to borrow money to open the store. Tricia made a token investment of four hundred dollars or so, which she eventually lost when the store went bust."

Melissa, dressed as before, came out of the house carrying a martini glass, which she put at Pankow's elbow. He mumbled automatic thanks and turned a page in his magazine, paying her no more attention than he would have given to the paper cover on a floppy disk. She went away again.

I asked Cora, "Did Deirdre leave town?"

"Technically, yes. She opened another store on Third Street in Newport, just across the river. She has a studio upstairs, where she paints and heats a can of soup now and then."

"She and Tricia became an item?"

"She was Tricia's next step. I had introduced Tricia to another life-style—another world, another planet. Deirdre is—well—imposing, as you will discover if you intend to meet her. Tricia realized that she and I were not the only two lesbians in the world. She was ready to expand her horizons. You might say I stepped aside."

"When was that?"

"Sometime after the holidays, January."

"And Tricia died in March," I mused. "See any connection?"

"She and I weren't as close in those last months as we had been. I want to say she seemed happy, but that's a slippery term applied to Tricia. She was less despondent, less depressed than I had ever known her to be. That goes for her personal life. How things were with her husband and her family, I can't say."

I had run out of questions. I left Cora one of my cards and suggested I might have to come back for more information.

Before I entered the freeway again, I stopped at a McDonald's for another coffee to go. In the parking lot I took out Tricia's suicide note and read through it once more.

18

BECAUSE THE PARK BENCHES in Cincinnati didn't look particularly comfortable, I decided it was time to think of shelter for the night and I chose the University area as a logical hub for my activities. My travel guide listed a hotel called Vernon Manor, where I headed. The lobby had autographed photos of celebrities who had stayed there, among them Jack Webb. That settled it. I registered and learned how much it cost and wondered how Webb had afforded it on a sergeant's pay.

When the bellhop had deposited me and my bags in my room, I treated myself to a long-overdue session in the bathroom. Afterwards, I spread Monk's Cincinnati map out and found the city of Newport at the bottom of the page on the Kentucky side of the river. Its street plan was simple enough. Numbered streets ran east-west, the numbers rising as they moved south from the river. Third Street was on the waterfront, with Monk's bold red circle directing me to Deirdre's studio-store-apartment. The map promised that the I-471 would deposit me in her neighborhood.

A few years ago Newport and Covington, the cities rubbing shoulders next door to the west, had been wide-open gambling resorts for Cincinnatians with a taste for vice, who thought sin was something else if you partook in another jurisdiction. I wasn't sure how much stock to put in the claims that reform administrations have cleaned things up over there, and I wasn't about to spare the time to investigate matters. I knew that in the old days the Mob had franchised Kentucky operations through its bases in Youngstown and Warren, which are satellites of the Cleveland organization, which brings to mind some boys from the old neighborhood—Shondor Birns, Danny Green, the Licavoli brothers, Jimmy (the Weasel) Frattiano, and John T. Scalish—many of whom have passed to their rewards in exploding Cadillacs. Their association with the locals in Northern Kentucky—with connections to Vegas and the West Coast—must have been something to see. The Godfather Meets the Good Ol' Boys, Mafiosi and Redneck linking arms to march forward to the Brotherhood of Profits.

Thoughts about those matters were in my mind when the freeway dumped me out onto Third Street and I began looking for the address of Deirdre Leminaux. Steamboat Gothic, with occasional touches of wrought-iron French Quarter design, was the prevailing style along the riverfront, further proof that the pull of gravity is toward the Gulf of Mexico. Most of the places could have been in Hannibal or New Orleans without great disruption to the ecology. Here they were falling into disrepair, paint peeling and porches collapsing. I found Deirdre's place, a house with the sign ART SHOP painted in elaborate scrollwork. When I had parked and locked my car, I walked up to it to read the CLOSED sign in the window.

An outside staircase led to the second floor, which had a landing and a door at its top. I climbed there and knocked. Time passed but my persistence paid off. The door was yanked open angrily. "This is my work time. I do not wish to be disturbed."

Cora had warned me she would be imposing. Deirdre was a black woman who, even in old gym shoes, matched my six-one height. Her age could have been almost anything, as low as her mid-twenties or beyond forty. She wore a sweatshirt and jeans, both spattered with paint, and had her hair done in a barely effeminate version of a flat-top. Her eyes warned: Don't cross me.

"I'm sorry about that. I only got a lead to you a little while ago." I gave her one of my cards.

She took it and held it in a hand with short yellow nails and dots of paint. "I have no business with Gilbert Disbro, Private Investigator."

"My business concerns the late Tricia Gault."

Plucked eyebrows rose. "Really? The whole sleazy world of private investigators must find her fascinating."

"John Monk found it so fascinating he died."

The news bulletin held her interest enough to keep her from slamming the door in my face. "Small loss to the world."

"Probably smaller than the loss of Tricia," I conceded. "That's my whole purpose being here."

"I have better things to do."

My wingtip in the door kept it from closing. "You're not

being very smart about this. I'm going to keep pestering you until you either talk to me or call the cops to have me hauled away. Do that and you'll be tied up for the next three or four hours giving statements, during which time you won't get any work done. But talk to me now for a few minutes, and I'll be out of your hair."

Deirdre considered the relative inconvenience of her options and showed me an expression that was ready to take up the challenge. "It could be an interesting test of wills."

"A bad contest for you. Even if you win, you lose."

"I will grant you fifteen minutes." She would always need to set the rules.

Without agreeing to a time limit, I stepped through the door and followed her into the living room. At least one wall had been sacrificed to make it what it was. The furniture was grouped on a rug in the center of the hardwood floor, with a counter at the far end dividing off the kitchenette. The real conversation piece, however, was toward the front of the building where a two-step-high dais sat in front of a window that curved up into part of the roof, like the wall and ceiling of a greenhouse. That dais was the spot where she did her painting. An easel had been set up there on a square of visquine holding her work in progress.

Based on my acquaintance with her at the door, I had been prepared for lots of leather, whips, and handcuffs, but not for this. The greenhouse window gave a panoramic view of the Cincinnati skyline with Riverfront Stadium in the foreground like a concrete doughnut. Samples of her work were on the walls and on the floor, tilted against the walls. Half of them were detailed pen-and-ink sketches of buildings done in draftsman's realism. I recognized the Carew Tower and a hall I had seen on the university campus. If I had been more familiar with Cincinnati, I probably would have recognized more places, many of which were stately old homes with interesting touches. There were some oil portraits, a couple of them elderly men in business suits who should have been hung in the lobby under the caption "Our Founder." Still another was a wide canvas of the skyline as seen from Deirdre's window.

She let me follow her up onto the dais where I had a peek at her work in progress. Maybe the stories I have heard about artists guarding their unfinished masterpieces have been exaggerated. Deirdre would not have been shy about telling me if I had been casting my eyes on forbidden subjects. This one was a square canvas on which she had been painting lines, vertical and horizontal, of varying widths and colors crossing one another like the pattern in a tartan blanket.

"Time is ticking away," she informed me as she picked up her brush.

"You're prolific in a variety of styles," I noted, using up about every buzzword I had stored in my art vocabulary.

"It requires a tremendous amount of discipline to budget time."

Wondering if she had ever been a DI in the Marine Corps, I let fly with a screwball: "Alan Gault still has that portrait of Tricia you painted. Two days ago I saw it in his house in Cleveland Heights."

She stopped with the tip of her paintbrush a sixteenth of an inch from the canvas. "I gave that to him after the funeral. He tried to pay me for it, but I refused. Tricia was dead, out of my life, and accepting money for it would have been like taking money from the man who hauls away your garbage." Her voice sounded false when honest emotion crept in. She would always have to add a postscript of hard-nosed philosophy.

"Anyway, who would want to pay good money for a portrait that looks like it faded in the wash."

Her head snapped around, colored strobe lights blinking in her eyes, mouth opening to defend her Art. Before she could say anything, something about me registered on her, telling her I was only trying to get a rise. "I saw Tricia in the process of being formed, no sharp edges developed yet." She turned back to her easel.

"If she was still forming, why did she kill herself?"

"Anomie. You'll find it in Durkheim."

"Durkheim's thesis was that people kill themselves when every other option is closed off."

She hesitated again with the brush teasing the canvas and looked inquiringly at me. "Do I detect a suggestion that you may have once read a book?"

"It was on the assigned list at private-eye school. Now that the government has started to regulate everything, they make us go to school. There are a few of us who can actually read and write—which is better than the public schools can claim. Were all of Tricia's options closed off?"

"It's not always the facts of the case. It's how the person perceives the facts. Tricia was torn by what appeared to be a conflict with no resolution. When we met, she was coming off an affair with—another woman."

"Cora Pankow," I supplied to let her know she didn't need to guard her tongue.

"Yes, Cora had inducted Tricia into a new life-style that was totally at odds with every notion her previous life had taught her. She had found satisfactions in lesbianism she had never found in abstinence or marriage, yet she could not shake off the Puritan ethic in her that taught anything pleasurable must be wrong."

Deirdre had picked up an edger, the same tool a house painter would use to keep wall paint off the woodwork. She used it to draw a straight horizontal line across the canvas.

"Is that playing by the rules?" I asked.

Deirdre grasped my meaning after a few seconds' pause. "Did you think I drew all those lines freehand? An artist uses whatever tools help him bring out his concept. Didn't you know that the Sistine Chapel was a sophisticated paint-by-numbers job? Do you object to a book because it was written with a word processor instead of a quill pen?"

"Couldn't you convince Tricia about the advantages of the new life?"

"My mission was to bring order and discipline to her life." She wiped excess paint off the edger and applied the tool to a vertical red line this time. "She was drifting aimlessly, leading what amounted to a double life. I tried to show her that continuing along those lines would require strict management of her time, exactly the kind of discipline she was not prepared for. The alternative, of course, was to make a clean break with her past. I do not permit smoking in my presence, much less in my own house."

I put the cigarette back in the pack and the pack back in my pocket, feeling an instant craving to reach for it. "Suppose she did. Where would she have gone?"

"Straight to me. I offered her a very business-like proposition. I wanted her to manage the store downstairs, while I devoted myself to painting. She could have drawn a salary better than she could have expected in the business world, and I would have let her live with me." She completed the vertical line and turned to me. "I thought the deal had been made but she killed herself."

The words ratcheted something in my mind. "Have you ever seen Tricia's suicide note?"

Her eyes clouded over. "What note?"

Out came my faithful photocopies. Deirdre put her tools aside, took the pages, and settled onto a high stool where a model might have perched. She read each page slowly, moving it to the rear when she was done so that they ended in same order.

"The police tell me the handwriting has been tested and proved to be Tricia's."

Deirdre nodded, not disputing that point. She read the pages a second time, as if searching for something she had overlooked. "It doesn't say anywhere that she intends to kill herself."

"That's right."

Deirdre read the opening words from Page One. " 'What I am about to do may surprise you.' " She went to another page. " 'Ultimate Act of Defiance.' " All that could just as well mean leaving him and coming to work for me."

"It could."

"But if that's what it meant, she intended to go on living."

"Maybe she was so confused she wrote it so it could be interpreted both ways," I suggested. "After it was written, she decided to end it all."

Deirdre went back through the text, shaking her head. "She rambles. She dances all around the subject, but she doesn't seem confused. There's nothing scratched out, nothing squeezed in between the lines. Whatever her intentions, her mind was made up when she wrote this."

I shrugged. "The coroner called it suicide."

"Bullshit." The full import of her word came to her. "If it wasn't suicide, that means someone killed her."

I took my copy of the note back. "I don't see any way to call it an accident."

Deirdre got up and paced back to her easel, then to her window, and then back across the visquine toward her living room. She stopped at the edge of the dais and spun back to me. "The investigation simply has to be reopened. How does one go about doing that?"

"You need proof."

"The note—"

"—is open to interpretation," I finished for her. "Besides, there's a tough hurdle to get over. The way the rope bit into her neck shows she was alive when she was hanged. I have to agree with the coroner on that one. Without marks of violence on her body, how can you imagine she was forced into it?"

"She was drugged."

I shook my head. "No drugs." I waited to see if she would say more.

Instead she walked back over to her window to look out on the view of Cincinnati. She stood looking at it a long time, arms folded, her back to me. When she did speak, it was none of the words I had expected. She pointed to a spot left of the Carew Tower.

"That's the west side, the black ghetto, where I was raised. Do I need to go into what conditions are like over there? Garbage? Rats? Drugs? Fights? Rage? You name it, it has it, if your subject is bad. Conventional wisdom tells you someone raised there doesn't have a chance. Still, there are exceptions like the little girl who one day sees the sun slanting down an alley and shining off the broken windows. At that angle for a few minutes, despite everything, the girl recognizes a glimmer of beauty. She wants to freeze that instant forever. Intuitively she has already learned a great lesson— that if an object of beauty can be found in such an unlikely place, there must be millions of bits like this one out there in the world. If only she can learn how you freeze that beauty, she can start capturing those instants and when she has enough of them, she can surround herself with them and block out all the ugliness she hates."

Deirdre turned back from the window to stare at me.

"How does she go about it? By discipline, by determination, by study, by hard work. All that makes her different from her friends. So be it. She will be different. Normal sex drives? They can get you in trouble, get you pregnant. Then be abnormal. You can't get pregnant if you fulfill your destiny with other women. Study, work, practice your art, get somewhere. Do you like my autobiography so far?"

"Do you?" I countered.

She thought about it. "Yes. It worked out fine, until I met someone as bad off in her own way as I was. I tried to help her, to support her, to depend on her. Goddamn it, I loved her! I thought she would come to me. I had visions of happiness. I waited for her that whole afternoon, but she didn't show up. And then I heard she was dead. I hated her for killing herself. It was proof that she didn't love me enough, or perhaps I hadn't loved her enough. We failed somehow, so I could hate her and go on. Now you tell me she didn't kill herself and there is not one thing we can do about it. How do you expect me to feel?"

There was nothing I could think to say, so I kept quiet.

Deirdre held herself together by breathing deeply, keeping the quiver in her voice from breaking out into something more. When she could trust herself to speak again, she said, "Your fifteen minutes are up."

19

THE HUMID AIR along the river bottom had been causing sweat to soak through my undershirt and shirt for most of the day. Back in my room, I stripped and made for the shower where I could rinse myself clean. When I was done, I stood by my window in my robe, toweling my hair, and looked down at rush-hour traffic clogging the streets. Six o'clock on a Friday. Helen and I went out to dinner on Friday evenings as part of the unconscious routine people establish to bring order to their lives. There was no reason for choosing Friday over any other night except that it was the end of her work week. It would have made as much sense for her to come home and collapse, maybe waking up for a late-night snack. My work was so irregular that I had no sense that one day of the week was different from any other. If anything, I did more on weekends than the rest of the week. Still, our Friday ritual had developed and I tried to observe it.

Thoughts of Helen brought with them twinges of guilt over my escapade with Arlene. I could kid myself into believing it had been done in the line of duty, playing along with her to find out where it would lead, like accepting a down payment on a bribe to collect evidence. Bullshit! I had been a horny and willing participant, and I had carelessly risked a relationship that means more to me than a hundred Arlenes. They call that a character flaw. I flopped down on the bed, ready to drift off to sleep after shortchanging myself last night, but fought it. When I began to feel as if I were balancing bricks on my eyelashes, I swung my feet over the side of the bed and dialed Helen's number. She answered on the second ring, home to cook her own meal that evening. It was only later, when I settled my bill, that I realized we talked for over a half hour. I can't remember all that we said—only the usual how are you and what have you been doing. I remember only how it ended.

"Hurry back," Helen urged. "I never knew my bed could seem so huge and empty."

"Tomorrow night," I promised, "you will have a deprived and lustful male under your covers."

I hung up feeling more shitty than ever. Arlene had been my first dalliance since I had started living with Helen nearly a year ago, which was a better record than I had maintained when I was married, but I'd been a cop then with all the temptations and opportunities that hang on a badge. We had been separated before, when I had gone to some distant city chasing down a bail jumper, but I had never gone looking for strange women on those occasions. Arlene had come on strong, of course, because it had suited her purposes to keep me occupied by seducing me. None of which had kept me from enjoying it as much, if I were any judge, as she had. Enough thinking about it would convince me the whole thing had been meaningless. No point in bringing it up to Helen.

I unfolded Monk's map once more and checked off the places he had marked. I had visited them all but the one on Colerain that represented Arlene's condominium. She had abandoned it when she had sold out her business and moved to Cleveland. Had anyone mentioned how she had disposed of the condo? I couldn't recall anything one way or the other. I decided it would be a place to visit before I left town. I put on clean underwear and a fresh blue button-down shirt, climbed into my same tan suit, and set out to find a meal.

On Ludlow I found a place billing itself as a family restaurant with no liquor license and plastic-topped tables. I never learned to trust a place that has to hide its tables under a cloth. When I had washed down the veal cutlet with enough coffee to offset the drowsiness from the weight of food in my stomach, I continued north on Ludlow until it connected with Colerain, which led me a winding course through the hills. Housing along it was a mixture, private homes interspersed with apartment villages. I watched the addresses until I found a sign:

HAWTHORN ESTATES
CONDOMINIUM FOR SALE
INQUIRE MGR.

According to the address I had got from the police report, Arlene's unit number had been 17. In front of that unit was a patch of grass the size of a card table with a For Sale sign stuck in it. The buildings in this development were actually duplexes, each with its own garage. There were three stories, the main floor half a flight up and the basement half-submerged, with a small balcony as high as my head beside the front door. The name-plate slot on the mailbox was blank. For the hell of it, I rang the bell and got no answer.

When I was getting into my car again, I glanced back up at Unit 17. A sliding glass patio door opened onto the balcony, making a picture window that was covered with a heavy drape. As I turned my head that way, the drape fell guiltily back into place.

Well.

I started my car and drove out of sight of Unit 17. At Unit 16 next door, I backed my car into a *Guests Only* space that allowed me to see the front of Unit 17 and the drive leading to it. I waited, smoking and considering my next move. The humid day was building toward a rainstorm and the gathering clouds were shortening the day. Still no lights on inside 17, not even the blue glow of a television set.

No more than fifteen minutes passed that way before a blue Fiat, with Cuyahoga County plates and a woman at the wheel, came down the drive and stopped in front of the garage to 17. The woman, Arlene, got out and lifted the garage door by hand. Her Genie was probably in her own car back in Cleveland. She returned to the Fiat, drove it into the garage, and got out again to close the overhead door. Before she could do it, I was standing there. She gasped, clinging to the garage door for support.

"You forgot to leave me money for your share of our motel room in Fort Wayne," I reminded her.

Two seconds passed while Arlene swallowed and brought herself under control. "After the use we got out of it? I didn't think it would be necessary."

"Shall we go inside and discuss it?"

"I have groceries in the car." She took out two paper bags from Convenient and led me to the entrance into the condo. There she paused, needing to fish her keys out of her purse. I took the grocery bags, while she opened the door and allowed me to walk ahead of her into the kitchen.

Across the narrow room was another doorway into the living room. Alan Gault was standing in it, leveling his Python on me. "Don't move," he said, because that was the next line a scriptwriter would have used.

I didn't. Coming through the door with my hands full had been taking a chance, but I was counting on it having a calming effect on Gault. Forcing my way in could have provoked him into a foolish move.

"Turn around," he ordered. "Put those bags on the counter."

"You just told me not to move," I pointed out.

"Do as I say."

"I'd like to but which one am I supposed to believe?"

He jiggled the revolver in his left hand. "Believe that. Now turn around."

"For God's sake, Alan," Arlene started to say.

I turned around and put the groceries on the counter.

"Lean up against the sink," Gault ordered.

Ignoring us, Arlene took a quart of milk out of one of the bags and set it on a shelf in the refrigerator, then turned on the lights to chase away the dim twilight and give Gault a clearer target. While I leaned on the sink, Gault gave me a superficial and unprofessional pat-down. When he found nothing, he stepped back. He couldn't have overlooked anything larger than an AK47.

"You can relax now," Gault told me.

I hadn't been tense but I faced him now. He still held the muzzle on me. "Where's Brandon?" I asked.

Gault debated with himself before he decided to answer me. "Upstairs. In bed. Asleep."

Arlene passed between us, distributing items to the shelves where she wanted them, her bracelets clinking with the movements of her arms. I said to Gault, "Why don't you put that piece away, Professor, and leave the menacing to Ted De Corsia? He was much better at it."

Gault had the good sense to realize he had been miscast. "We'll go into the living room." He backed up, inclining his head to signal me to follow him. When I did, he pointed me to a love seat. "Sit there."

I obeyed. Gault snapped on a light and settled into an easy chair facing me, placing the Colt on the end table beside his left hand. The living room was L-shaped, bending around a staircase, with a dining table before another patio door looking onto a redwood deck and the back yard. Letting him see what I was doing, I got out my cigarettes and shook one loose.

"Arlene tells me you're a private detective that Monica hired to find me."

"It looks like another success for my illustrious record." I lit my cigarette and blew smoke in his direction. The cloud curled back on itself before it got there and drifted away.

"So now go away. Go back to Cleveland and tell Monica where I am, as long as she's sworn to secrecy."

"What are you going to do? Hide out here the rest of your life?"

"It's a safe harbor for the time being." Gault's drawn face belied his claim. He looked more like a man in the middle of a storm-tossed sea.

"Your father-in-law will find you eventually. He intends to take Brandon away from you by force, legal or otherwise."

"Then it has to be extra-legal. He has no grounds."

"He has a weapon, one you might not be aware of. How's Brandon? Still catatonic?"

"He's not his usual bubbly self, but he's been through a lot. It takes time."

The noise from the kitchen of Arlene banging cupboard doors as she put things away had ended. She stepped into the doorway.

"Maybe more than you think. Do you know he's been abused?"

"We discovered it when we gave him a bath." Gault's hands squeezed his knees, causing the muscles in his forearms to bulge. He was having trouble repressing rage. "What happened?"

"Your father-in-law has a theory on that. John Monk held him for nearly forty-eight hours after the kidnapping. Monk had some suggestions of child molesting in his past."

"That asshole! I'll kill him for that!" Gault paused while his words rang. "He's lucky he's already dead!"

"Hammond's theory is that Monk abused him and that later Brandon got hold of his gun and killed him."

"No." Gault shook his head. "It didn't happen like that! It couldn't! It—" The idea took hold of him then. He looked at me with wild eyes, then at Arlene, seeking denial. "My God!" He clasped a hand over his mouth and ran for the stairs. Seconds later the sound of retching came from the bathroom.

While he was gone, I picked up the Python, opened the cylinder, and dumped the rounds into my palm. Although the Python will handle .357s, Gault had loaded this one with .38 Specials, round-nosed 200-grain loads. I dumped them in my side jacket pocket, replaced the gun on the end table, and sat again. Arlene had watched without comment.

Upstairs a toilet flushed and Gault returned wiping his

face with a hand towel. He looked like a man who had barely pulled through a long sickness. "Sorry." He slumped in the chair and rested his face on the towel in his hands. "I won't believe it."

"You half-believe it already, and it's making you useless, and that's Hammond's weapon. It's working in his favor now. He's planted the doubt. He knows you won't let Brandon be dragged into a murder case, not even to be questioned. You'd cover up first."

Gault looked up from the towel. "He would be right. There's no reason to believe Brandon is the only one who could have murdered Monk. Anyone could have walked into that apartment. Why I was even there."

Now it was my turn to show shock. I managed to avoid upchucking. "When?"

"Saturday, late in the afternoon."

My one reason for eliminating Gault from the list of suspects had been the unlikelihood he would have known enough to find Wyckoff's apartment. Fighting to keep my voice level, I asked, "How did you get there?"

"Long story." His voice was too weary to try recounting it for my benefit.

"Professor, the last week of your life has not been accounted for. It's best you start explaining yourself."

"Who would care?"

"Detective Manuel Agosta of Cleveland Homicide, for one. He'd like to be able to put you in the apartment in time to murder Monk."

"He was dead when I got there." Gault examined my unrelenting expression and decided to explain himself. "When Brandon disappeared a week ago Wednesday, I went frantic. I was running all over Cleveland trying to find him. God, I can't even remember all the places I went. By Thursday I knew I was wasting my time. I knew the Hammonds must have taken him. I started out for Fort Wayne. Along the way, I simply ran down. I hadn't had any sleep for almost two days, so I stopped at a motel near Toledo. Friday morning I drove on to Fort Wayne and went to the Hammond house. No one was there. I wasted most of the day trying to find them in Fort Wayne, and finally I realized they must be in Cleveland. I started home."

I had visions of Hammond and Gault passing each other on the trips. "Back in Cleveland I stopped at my house Friday night. I stayed there long enough to pack a few clothes and pick up my gun." Mentioning it made him look at the end table at his elbow. He was satisfied to see its ventilated rib was attached. "On Saturday morning, I stopped by my office at the university to see if anyone had left any messages there. Damon Herlihy, who shares the office with me, was there, sleeping off a drunk from the night before. I woke him and tried to question him. He babbled something about a student who had tried to go through my desk. He said he wrote down the student's information in his notebook. I found the notebook in his pocket and got the name, Ted Wyckoff."

"Herlihy told me he had never seen you."

"I'm not surprised," Gault said. "Drunk as he was, he probably thought he'd dreamed it, or maybe forgot it. After I got Wyckoff's name, I wasted a lot of time because the records office is closed on Saturday. Finally I located someone—a secretary who owed me a favor—and convinced her to loan me her keys. I dug out Wyckoff's record and ran off copies. Then I had to return the key to the secretary. Anyway, it was late in the afternoon by the time I reached Wyckoff's apartment on Fleet Street. No one answered my knock, but I noticed the door had not been shut quite tight enough for the lock bolt to catch. I pushed it open and found—the dead man."

More traffic had passed through Wyckoff's apartment than crosses the Main Avenue Bridge. I considered Gault's story and tried to figure out his place in line—after Wyckoff, who had come Saturday morning, and before Bobbie came Wednesday. "You searched the place?"

He nodded. "I was looking for some sign of Brandon. I didn't find anything but somehow I knew he'd been there. Intuition, I suppose you would call it, but also reasoning told me he must have been held there. Also, I knew that the dead man was not Wyckoff because I had seen his ID photo. That left me two questions to answer: Where was Wyckoff? Who was the dead man?

Other thoughts were filling my mind. What if Gault had been lying about what day he went to Wyckoff's apartment? His Python was the caliber of the murder weapon, but the 200-grain round-nosed bullets were all wrong for the damage done to Monk's head.

"Sunday was a waste," Gault was saying. "I checked into a downtown hotel, some fleabag, to be alone to make my plans. Monday I tried to locate Wyckoff by following his schedule, but obviously he was cutting class. I went to the library and searched through the *Reader's Guide* for every article I could find relating to kidnapping and child stealing. Then I would go to the periodical it came from. At last I came to an article on Monk John that had his picture with it. He was the dead man."

Gault's detective techniques had been more appropriate to scholarly research than investigations, but I was willing to grant him points for his efforts.

"Tuesday I followed Wyckoff's class schedule again and again he failed to show. I tried looking up his employment record and searching for him at those places. Wednesday was the same until I finally caught up with him at Ernie's. I accosted him and demanded to know where my son was. He was not cooperative. He had a file folder that he claimed came from Monk and had the lowdown on me. Later, I saw it was only a copy of the police report on Tricia's death. He kept waving the folder and—well—the whole situation degenerated into violence. We were still fighting when you arrived with Professor Scagnetti. After that, I realized I needed an ally and I went to Arlene."

The rest of it I had already doped out for myself. I got up and walked to the back patio where I could look out onto the wooded hillside behind the condos. While I stood there, lightning flashed, followed by thunder, and the saturated skies dumped on the world below. I turned from the window and came back to Gault, lighting a fresh cigarette.

"You can't let my father blackmail Alan into giving up his son," Arlene told me. "The poor boy is going to need all the psychological help he can get. First he sees his mother's suicide, then he's abused, then he kills. You must help."

Speaking to her but looking at him, I said, "I can't keep anyone from giving in to blackmail."

"Why do they keep after Brandon?" Gault complained. "Why can't they let us alone?"

"They want a Barbie doll to play with," Arlene answered him. "They want another mind to warp."

I said, "They want to use him to prove you killed your wife."

Gault looked at me as if I had spoken in a language he didn't understand. "That makes no sense at all. Tricia committed suicide."

"That's not set in cement," I told him. "Only a couple hours ago, I found out her note could have meant she was leaving to go live with her lesbian lover."

"Lesbian?" The notion was as outrageous to Gault as the idea of his son as a killer. Then, as he contemplated the upheavals in his life, one more was easier to accept. He fit it into place. "Cora Pankow."

"She started it but Tricia had moved on to another one."

"You could construct a hypothesis in which lesbianism would be only one more motive for suicide," Gault offered. "Besides, there is all the physical evidence that the coroner used to prove it was suicide."

"It only proves she died in the rope. It doesn't show how she got there." I swallowed and plunged into it. "Remember what Tricia was doing in the basement—the laundry. Near her body was a basket loaded with possible murder weapons—towels, sweatshirts, anything you want to name, which is something the gun haters in this country never understand. Suppose someone with a reason to kill her was there. They argued, Tricia turned her back, the killer grabbed a towel and strangled her from behind. I say behind because Tricia's face had turned white instead of red. The killer kept up the pressure until Tricia slumped unconscious, not dead. The killer realized the mistake. Maybe Tricia was gagging or the killer detected a heartbeat. Quick, the killer rigged the noose over the pipe—the clothesline was right there. The killer lifted Tricia, half-walking her, stuck her head in the noose, and let the rope finish the job. The important thing is that being strangled with the cloth leaves no marks. Because she was alive when her head went in the noose, the marks of the rope were consistent with suicide."

"Who would do such a thing?" Gault asked.

"Besides you?" I looked across the room. "Arlene, because she wanted Tricia out of the way, reverse English on your motive. Cora Pankow, because Tricia had jilted her. Edward Pankow, jealousy over his wife. Deirdre Leminaux, maybe because Tricia decided to withdraw from a business deal they had. I'm only mentioning people I met today."

"I meant, who would know enough to do what you described? I only half understand what you're talking about. I didn't know even one-tenth of these technicalities a year ago. Arlene didn't, nor Cora, nor Edward, nor anyone else who isn't a professional in homicide matters. There is only one man with that kind of expertise in criminal matters, Wesley Hammond."

"Wrong premise," I told him. "You can't assume Tricia's death passed for suicide because the killer was so expert. The crime worked because the killer was an amateur and there was no planning ahead. If it had been planned by a professional, the killer would have placed the knot of the noose at the back of her head. Then there would have been no question."

Gault wiped his face with his towel again, expending more thought. "I didn't do it."

"No comment at this time," I said.

"There are circumstances around Tricia's death that should be investigated, as well as what happened to John Monk. What do you charge?"

"Twenty dollars an hour, plus expenses. But I'm not sure that's relevant. Monica Brodbeck is my client. She hired me to find you, which I've done. Maybe, when she hears what I've uncovered so far, she'll want me to continue. Maybe she'll be afraid to go ahead. Either way, she gets first chance." Saying that much was one of the hardest statements I had ever made. Unless you've been caught up in the forward momentum of a breaking case, you can't know how hard it is to jump off.

"Look, I'll pay you for what you've done so far. Or reimburse Monica if that's the proper procedure," Gault promised. "I want you to stay on the case to protect Brandon and me from Hammond and to find out what is really behind this all."

"Careful of what you're buying. You might be paying me to dig up evidence that will put you in the Death House."

"You won't find any because it doesn't exist."

I looked at Arlene. "Or someone close to you."

"I have nothing to fear," Arlene assured me.

No one seemed interested in stopping me, but it wouldn't be the first time a grandstand play had been made to divert suspicion. "Is your phone still connected?" Arlene nodded and I said to Gault, "Call Monica after I leave. Don't tell her anything except you're alive and well. Also tell her you'll be in Cleveland tomorrow by 8 P.M. to leave Brandon in her care."

"What?" They both sang the word in harmony.

"Hammond will be in Cleveland, but he doesn't know Monica exists, does he? You got an idea of a place where Brandon would be safer?"

Before I left, I returned Gault's six rounds. Outside, the thunderstorm had slacked off to a drizzle. I dashed to my car and drove back to my hotel. The downpour had left the streets looking more like creeks with pools collecting at the bottoms of hills.

From my room I put through a call to Monica's number. Gault had already talked to her and she was ecstatic, willing to pay AT&T top dollar to tell me how great a guy I am. I told her I already knew that and asked her to write down Helen's address on Bridge Avenue. When she had read it back to me, she asked, "What is the point?"

"Meet me there tomorrow at four o'clock. We're going to have lots of interesting things to discuss."

20

AFTER BREAKFAST in the hotel coffee shop the next morning, I set out for Cleveland. I had managed to read the *Cincinnati Enquirer* while eating, my first newspaper in a couple days, and had found the people elected to represent me had not done irreparable damage to the Republic while my back was turned. Feeling generally good, I headed north on Interstate 71, which would carry me northeast on a diagonal slash across the state to within a few blocks of Helen's house.

The dial on my car radio marked my progress. Leaving Cincinnati, it was tuned to WLW until, approaching Columbus a hundred miles later, it moved to WBNS. I passed through Columbus, a curious city that has no reason to exist except as a stage setting for the state capital and Ohio State University, and stopped for a carry-out lunch outside Delaware, twenty miles north. Beyond Delaware, I began picking up WWWE, a bit of home. The same storm system that had drenched Cincinnati last night had been ahead of me on the same route until Ashland, where I overtook it. I had to turn on my headlights and wipers and slow to the lower sixties. The rest of the trip was a bummer.

Helen greeted me with a hug when I came in the door, not minding rubbing against my wet clothes. If I had let it go, it could have been a real homecoming celebration, but I knew Monica would be arriving soon. I was upstairs unpacking my suitcase when Helen called me to let me know I had company. I came down to find Monica already settled with Helen in the study.

"This man is wonderful," Monica announced when I walked in. She bounced out of her chair to throw her arms around my neck and give me a kiss on the cheek. "You don't know how he's set my mind at ease. I hope you appreciate him."

"He's going to be insufferable for a week," Helen predicted. "I'll fix the coffee."

While she was gone, I steered Monica back into her chair and settled myself at Helen's work station in the corner, a desk and a table for her word processor. It's all ergonomically designed except that her desk faces the wall, so it's nearly impossible to adapt it as an office.

"I haven't had a chance to put any of my results in writing," I explained to Monica. "You will get a written report, but it's a couple days down the road."

"The only report I was interested in was the phone call I got from Alan last night." Her eyes searched for the clock on the wall. "Only four more hours until he gets here."

"Arlene's with him," I said.

"Oh." Monica bit her lip and looked down at her hands, which were wrestling one another for control of her emotions. "The important thing is that he and Brandon are back." Somehow she didn't make me believe that was the most important thing in her life.

"I'm ready to give my oral report now, but maybe there are parts of it you'd rather not hear. Maybe you'd rather forget the report."

"Let me hear it." She had to know where Arlene would fit into the picture.

Helen returned with our coffee. With Monica's permission I allowed Helen to sit in so I would only have to say this once. I started then with an account of all that had happened since I had dropped Monica off Wednesday morning. Not quite all. I did some fancy tapdancing around the night in the Fort Wayne motel, managing to give the impression that Arlene had checked into a separate room and stayed there. Even to me my voice sounded shameful with the lies. Despite such ambiguities and omissions, it took the best part of an hour to tell it all in enough detail for Monica to understand the salient points. By telling it again, I was also helping myself organize my own thoughts on the case. I concluded:

"So you understand why we're asking you to watch Brandon. We want him someplace where Hammond can't find him. You're taking a risk, but your best protection is Hammond's ignorance. Since he's never heard of you, he won't start looking for you."

"I understand," Monica agreed, "and I'm willing to take care of him, of course. But is that best for Brandon? Shouldn't he be under a doctor's care?"

"I don't know," I said honestly. "Putting him under a doctor's care now is like pleading him guilty to murder."

"They would never prosecute an eight-year-old," Helen

said, doubt staining the edges of her confidence. "Would they?"

"Not the way they would an adult. More likely, he would be institutionalized several years, while the shrinks decide how much his id has been warped."

The two women exchanged looks as they translated my terminology back into educationese. Monica finally said it. "The fact that we should face is that a period of institutionalization might be the best way to help Brandon."

I looked at the grounds in my coffee mug. "The problem with everybody being so damned eager to help Brandon is that they forget to ask the hard questions."

"What is that supposed to mean?" Helen asked.

"An eight-year-old makes one hell of a fall guy."

Monica looked puzzled while Helen gasped softly. "Do you doubt that Brandon killed Monk?"

"I think it would be nice to look into it before we send the kid over."

"You have something." Helen's inflection made it a statement.

"The evidence at the scene of the crime has been tampered with so goddamn often," I pointed out, "I can't be sure of anything. When I was in the apartment, Monk's holster was on a high shelf where Brandon couldn't have reached it, certainly not in the split-second timing that would have been necessary for Hammond's theory to work."

The women took a few seconds absorbing that much and drawing the conclusion. Monica got to put it into words. "Then Brandon couldn't have shot Monk."

"If the evidence I saw was pure," I added. "Even if Brandon didn't shoot Monk, he saw who did it. You're going to be with him the next few days, Monica. You could try drawing him out."

"And end up driving him deeper into his shell."

"I wasn't asking you to give him the third degree. Be alert in case he brings something up. Be open, ready to listen. Maybe something he sees on television will start a train of thought." I picked up my cup and carried it out to the kitchen for a refill.

When I returned, the two women were discussing studies by sundry doctors who had investigated trauma and the preadolescent. Helen was pulling a couple books off the shelf, while Monica searched the footnotes and indexes for references to scholarly journals. Such is life when you find yourself bookended between teachers. I sat down to sip coffee and wait for an opening.

"What next, Monica?" I asked when the chance came. "I found Gault, so my job is done. Do you want me to stop or keep on?"

She flapped her arms helplessly and appealed to Helen. "I don't know what to do."

"You should know that Gault is offering to reimburse you for what you've paid so far and keep paying me."

"Then it's settled," Monica decided.

"I'd rather have you for a client," I told her, "even if you're using Gault's money."

"Why?"

"Because I'm still not sure he didn't kill his wife. If the time comes when I have to turn him in, it leads to all kinds of conflicts. With you as the client, I don't have any."

"Alan never harmed anybody." Monica reconsidered all I had said and reached a conclusion. "Look into Tricia's suicide, by all means. Clear the clouds from over Alan's head."

I got out one of my contract forms and made it out so my mission was "investigate circumstances surrounding the death of Patricia Hammond Gault." Monica signed it, and I filed it.

She was still eager to see Gault again despite the news I had given her about Arlene. Our business concluded, she headed for the door, loaded down with books from Helen's shelf. When I had seen her out, I shut the door and faced Helen. "See what you get me into?"

"I had no idea it would lead to so many complications. What do you have in mind now?"

"Ted Wyckoff. I never got a chance to question him the way I should. He took papers out of Monk's motel room that were supposed to have something to do with Tricia's death. Monk was at least thinking of using what he found to blackmail Gault, but Gault claims the papers were only the police report on Tricia's suicide. Maybe and maybe not Wyckoff will be able to tell me there's more to it."

Helen stepped up to me, sliding her hands up my chest, over my shoulders and around my neck, bringing her face close to mine. "Tomorrow?"

"Tonight."

"I have a contract," she told me, our noses nearly touching, "the terms of which guarantee me I will not have to sleep alone tonight. You wouldn't want me to be forced to hire some high-priced law firm to enforce it."

"A couple hours should do it. You're welcome to come along."

"I'll busy myself with some lecture notes until you get back."

Before I went upstairs, we spent some time sealing our bargain with affection. In our bedroom, I put on my tie and reached for my coat. Among the items I had unpacked was my Smith & Wesson Model 19 in its shoulder harness, lying on the foot of the bed. It had been with me through my travels, packed away because I had never been certain of what the laws were in the various jurisdictions I had passed through. When it might have been handy, it had been out of reach. I resolved not to let that happen again. When I put the rig on like a vest, the revolver rode upside down against my left ribs, balanced by the speedloaders attached to the strap on the opposite side. I pulled it out and checked the loads in the chambers, Plus P hollow points, a world away from the loads Gault carried. I tucked the piece back in my holster, put on my suit jacket, and picked up the phone.

Even on Saturday evening I got an answer at Moe Glickman's Bail Bonds. Weekends are the busy time in that business with people getting arrested and needing to reach a bondsman with their one allowable phone call. Although the office is closed, the answering service is there to reach someone in a hurry. The operator told me I had only one message. Wesley Hammond had called to let me know he was staying at the In-Towner Motor Inn on Superior. I copied down his number, depressed the cradle, and tapped it out, not surprised when Hammond's room did not answer. Even fundamentalists have to eat.

Downstairs again, I interrupted Helen in the study going over her notes. We kissed good-bye and I got my raincoat from the closet on the way out.

Rain was still pelting down remorselessly as I drove down West Twenty-fifth to Broadview to the apartment complex where Bobbie lived. No green Mustang was parked before her door and no lights showed in her apartment. I risked drowning as I trudged through the rain to ring her doorbell, getting no answer. Back in my car, I thought about a trip to Slavic Village to Wyckoff's apartment. Even if he had gone back there while I was out of town, he would have found a police seal on his door. Even if he had wanted to break the seal and try living in his old apartment before it had been fumigated, he would have been inviting arrest—

in which case I would have to look him up in the Justice Center.

None of which seemed likely. I turned on my dome light and looked in my notebook for the address of Bobbie's employer, Wally's Tavern on Snow Road in Parma. It was only a couple miles from where I sat, much closer than either of the other possibilities.

I headed there to see if Bobbie could tell me anything.

21

WALLY'S WAS HAVING a big Saturday night. The bar was stacked two deep, most of the tables had customers, and the game machines were crowded. The uniform of the day, for both men and women, seemed to be bowling shirts. They were a noisy bunch, drowning out the sound of the projection television with coarse jokes and shouts and laughter but keeping themselves a few notches short of rowdiness. The bartender was busy trying to service five more customers than he could handle, while two barmaids were sprinting from table to bar to booth.

I entered by the side door direct from the parking lot. If I had learned nothing else from my years on the police department, I had developed an instinct for sizing up the temper of a bar with only one foot across the threshold. That instinct told me Wally's was not a trouble spot. It might not score high on refinement, but you could leave the place with as many teeth as you brought in, unless you went out of the way to cause trouble. I hung my dripping raincoat on an aluminum coat tree and went to a vacant table in Bobbie's section.

It had been vacated not long ago. Empty beer bottles and glasses still littered its top. I watched Bobbie as she worked her way to me. She was easily the more efficient and popular of the two barmaids, joking with the patrons, fielding passes, moving quickly to the next table. Her uniform was a short cheerleader skirt and a boat-neck top that dipped low to reveal two of her attractions. When she reached me, she went to work cleaning off the debris of the last customers, emptying the ashtray and wiping off the ebony table top where interlocking rings had long ago embedded a permanent design like the pattern of a chain-link fence—all without looking at my face.

"What'll it be?"

I hadn't planned an answer for that one. My hesitation made her look up and the sight of me made her frown. "Where's Ted?" I asked.

Her reply was slow in coming as she wondered if she should answer at all. "He's supposed to be here at closing time to pick me up. He has my wheels again."

"Still hasn't got his transmission fixed?"

"Why should he bother when he's got me to borrow from? You ordering?"

"Scotch and water."

She left to get it. When she returned, I laid a five on the table. She gave me change and I gave her one of my cards. She read it and looked up at me. "Ted says he never heard of you. You took advantage of me when I didn't have my wits about me."

"We should talk."

"No way."

"I understand how you feel." I tried on a contrite expression. "When I saw you the other day, I didn't know how involved this all was. Ted's in more trouble than he could ever know."

Bobbie's eyes showed a weakening of her will. "Ted's troubles aren't mine."

"I understand. I hope that tomorrow, or three days down the road, you won't be kicking yourself because you wouldn't spare some time tonight."

Bobbie looked at my card again and put it in the pocket of her apron. "I'm due for a break. Hold on."

She made another sweep of her section to make sure all the customers had been served and turned in her tray at the bar. I sipped my scotch and waited for her to return with a drink of her own in her hand. "You're paying for it," she informed me as she put it on the table. She plucked two dollars out of my change and sat opposite me, closing her eyes in relief as weight left her feet.

"Where was Ted going tonight?"

"Wheeling and dealing. Where else?"

"What's he working on now?"

"Same as before, I guess. He doesn't explain it all to me. He only brags about how much he's going to make, only it never comes." She lit a cigarette and inhaled smoke deep into her lungs, treating me to the sight of her breasts swelling under her top.

"The cops been looking for him?"

She gave that one more consideration than it needed. "There was one, yesterday, who might have been a cop. A big guy with white hair cut in a buzz, maybe sixty years old. He never showed a badge but he acted like a cop. Like you."

I figured she had been describing Hammond. "What did he want?"

"To talk to Ted. They had a conversation outside the apartment in the parking lot for maybe five minutes. Then Ted got in the guy's car, a Wagoneer, and they took off somewhere. They were gone about an hour when I had to leave for work. All I know is that Ted was back home when I got off around two in the morning."

"Ted say what they talked about?"

"It had to have something to do with the Monk getting killed, didn't it?" She took a healthy swig of her drink and waited for my answer.

"Give Ted my card when you see him," I told her. "You can say I've been following the same trail as the Monk, and I'm willing to offer Ted the same deal he had. There should be enough in it for him to get his transmission fixed. Maybe even buy you a new car."

That impressed her. "Like I said, Ted will be here at closing time. That's one o'clock. You're welcome to wait, or come back."

The thought of sitting around a bar for five hours was too depressing to consider. One of the reasons I don't drink is that I get bored too fast in a bar. Besides, it would have meant passing up my homecoming treat with Helen. "There's always tomorrow. I'll catch you then."

I left my change on the table with my drink and took down my raincoat. Outside, I revved up my car to head back to Bridge Avenue. Cleveland was simply too big a place to go looking for Wyckoff on a nasty night like this. I thought of trying Hammond at his motel. If he had come to some kind of understanding with Wyckoff, he might know where to find him. The hell with it. Tomorrow would do.

One idea came to me as I drove up Ridge Road, a place to check that would require only a slight detour. I followed Ridge to the Denison intersection and took Denison to Lorain. That brought me to the vicinity of Ernie's Body Shop where Wyckoff and Gault had promoted their grudge match.

I approached the garage warily in the dark and rain, remembering the chuck holes in the alley and the miscellaneous auto parts scattered about. I parked farther away from the garage than I would have liked if I had been more sure of the terrain and got my disposable flashlight out of the glove box before I exited the car. Keeping the beam on the ground ahead of me, I approached the door, stepping around Bobbie's green Mustang.

Light was showing behind the translucent squares in the overhead garage door, maybe nothing more than the night light the owner had left on to discourage burglars. Or, laws being what they are these days, maybe it was there so the burglars wouldn't trip over something and sue the owner. Rain was matting my hair and running down my neck as I reached the walk-in door. I tapped on it lightly and then tried the knob, which was a straight handle. It worked and the door opened easily. Over the pounding of the rain, I detected the heavier, louder pounding of rock music from WMMS.

The walk-in door admitted me into a small office with a metal desk piled high with papers, bills stuck on a spike, fast-food wrappers, cigar butts in an ashtray the size of a fry pan, and other detritus I didn't catalogue. I moved my flashlight beam across a nude on the wall to a doorway leading into the service bays. Beside the door was a pair of signs:

WARNING: NO CUSTOMERS IN SERVICE AREA
NOTICE: WE DO NOT LOAN TOOLS

Duly warned, I passed through the portal onto the cement floor of the garage. The glow I had seen against the translucent windows had come from a soft-drink machine against the wall. There was a stronger light farther back, coming from a work lamp on a cord at the end service bay. The loud rock music came from one of the cars left there for service, a two-year-old Plymouth. I flashed my beam around it, finding no one under it or in it. Through the open driver's window I saw the keys in the ignition, turned to the first position to allow the radio to play and the battery to run down. I reached through and turned the switch off. Blessed silence in time to save the last membrane in my ear drums.

"Wyckoff!" The sudden silence allowed my word to echo back, —*off*.

I forged on down the line of service bays to the one at the end where the utility light hung above the open hood of a battered Camaro, which still showed its original yellow paint among the patches of bondo. Its right door had been replaced with a red one. Around its right headlight, parts of the torn fiberglas hung out like unraveled cloth. Its front tires had been removed, leaving it sitting down-sloping on its rims. In front of the car, a hook lay on the floor along with part of its slack chain that ran up to a pulley at the ceiling.

I walked around to the far side of the Camaro and there spotted the bottom half of a man's body jutting out from under the car on a wooden dolly whose wheels had collapsed inward. He had been wearing cowboy boots, jeans, a wide belt with a fancy silver buckle, and a checked shirt. I couldn't see more than that because the left front rim of the Camaro had sliced through his body like a buzz-saw blade six inches

above the belt line. Plenty of blood had leaked out to mingle
with the oil and grease stains on the floor. I got down on my
stomach and shined the flashlight beam under the car to the
victim's face. Ted Wyckoff had died with an expression of
"Oof!" frozen on his features as the metal had crashed down
on him.

Brushing dirt off my raincoat, I stood up and examined
the situation with the eye of an insurance adjuster trying to
decide how the accident had happened. The hook had been
used to raise the front half of the car. The chain ran up
through the block and tackle, across six feet of ceiling,
through a pulley and down to a hand-operated winch—a
large-scale model of the same apparatus that raises the net on
the tennis court. You set the hook under the car bumper and
turned the crank on the winch until it was as high as you
wanted. Then you pushed the locking lever down so that
teeth in the gear could not reverse. When you were done,
you moved the locking mechanism up and cranked the lever
in the opposite direction to let the car down gently. If you
didn't, it would crash.

Close examination showed that the gear teeth were worn
round and shiny and smooth from the years of use. It was
conceivable that Wyckoff had banged against the car while
he was working, causing the gear teeth to slip, popping the
lock up to Off, and letting the car crunch down on him.

It was also conceivable that a human hand had flipped the
lock up and let gravity do the rest.

I examined the footprints in the oily dirt on the cement
floor. There was no shortage of them, too many for my
limited skills. It would have taken an Apache tracker to sort
them all out. I studied the area around the winch, distinguishing some high-heeled prints that Wyckoff's cowboy
boots would have left there in any case. Beyond that incon-
clusive point, the confusion was too great for me to follow.

Touching Wyckoff's body told me nothing I couldn't have learned other ways—dead two or three hours with distinct rigor mortis. I already knew he had driven Bobbie to work that evening, and tensing of muscles at the instant of death like this one leads to pronounced rigor. I headed for the office where I expected to find a telephone under the clutter on the desk and then wondered, why bother? His body would be found when the place opened for business Monday morning. Let Ernie, or whoever came in, do the explaining to the police. If I had been sure that Manny Agosta would have responded to the call, I might have gone through with it. But Agosta was working first platoon, the day shift, unlikely to be around on a weekend evening. If the body turned up on his watch, Agosta would be quicker to connect the name of a man who had rented an apartment where a body had been discovered three days ago. Letting nature take its course that way would save me the hassle of trying to explain things I didn't understand myself.

Besides, I had personal reasons for wanting to rush home.

When I got there, I caught Helen indulging her secret vice—watching a taped episode of "Falcon Crest." She quickly shut off the VCR and I pretended I hadn't noticed. "Did you find Mr. Wyckoff?" she asked conversationally.

"He wasn't in a talkative mood."

My answer was vague enough to satisfy what little curiosity she had on the subject. We got around to celebrating my homecoming in a proper manner.

22

THE IN-TOWNER MOTOR INN, just east of the Innerbelt ravine on Superior, clung desperately to respectability while teetering on the brink of the scabrous. For that reason, it might have been a bargain if you didn't mind the noises of a hooker plying her trade in the next room. Church bells were ringing when I passed from the bright Sunday morning sunlight into the dim lobby to ask the desk clerk to ring Hammond's room. When that got no answer, I went into the coffee shop to wait.

It was a diner with its main entrance on Superior, its passage into the lobby only coincidental. I ordered myself a breakfast while I waited, reasonably sure where Hammond had gone. Something like a half hour elapsed while I downed a Western, watching the working girls who had lucked into all-night stands slipping out. Three of them who met in the lobby decided to come into the diner for coffee. They occupied stools at the counter from which they gave me curious glances until I shook my head. My attention was centered on the street.

A little before noon, Hammond showed with Esther on his arm. She had gussied herself up for the church services, wearing a pink dress with a matching pink pillbox hat and a plastic red flower on her bodice. She was carrying her Bible. Hammond, too, was in his Sunday-go-to-meeting clothes, a double-knit suit too tight for him. It occurred to me any suit would be too tight on him unless it was tailor-made.

I intercepted them in the lobby. "Don't you ever stay in your room?"

"We have been out to services," Esther told me, with the implication I could have employed my time to better advantage. She looked at the clothes I wore—pale blue jeans, a yellow shirt without a tie, a seersucker jacket—and reached a conclusion about my sinful nature. "You have not."

"Alas, I've been traveling." I turned my attention to Hammond. "Would you like to join me in the coffee shop? We can talk there."

"What say, Esther? Ready for some chow?"

She said she could eat, and we returned to my booth. I signaled the waitress and told her to put whatever they wanted on my bill, which encouraged them to order a full meal. I had more coffee. While we waited, I watched them seated side by side across the table from me. "Did you enjoy church services?" I asked sociably.

"Finding a church that will preach a literal interpretation of God's Word in a strange city is most difficult," Esther lectured me. "Furthermore, the word 'enjoy' hardly is appropriate to describe one's reaction to hearing God's message. The minister today was far too liberal in virtually everything he said. Are you affiliated with any sect?"

I think I surprised her with a truthful answer. "I was confirmed Lutheran."

Esther literally tried to push away from such close association with a semi-Papist. She looked out the window at the people passing on the sidewalk. "So many people who have not been to church on a Sunday morning."

"Thing you got to realize about a city like this," Hammond told her, "lots of them are Jews, except for the coloreds."

"At least," Esther concluded, "those three young ladies at the counter are dressed appropriately. It wouldn't surprise me to learn they had been teaching Sunday School."

Their food came then and I let them enjoy their free meal. When they were on their dessert, I decided it was safe to light a cigarette and open the conversation with the nearest thing I had to a bombshell. "Well, Wes, did you learn a lot from Ted Wyckoff?"

Hammond paused with a piece of apple pie three inches from his mouth. Instead of being surprised, he smiled and then bit the piece of pie off his fork. "You're on the ball."

"I had a description of the man who came to see him in a Wagoneer. It fit you."

"I was hoping to find out how much Monk had on Gault. Wyckoff lost it. He claims there was another man there at the time—twenty-five, six-one, one-eighty, blond with a mustache. Probably I could find someone in this room to fit that description."

"How did you get onto Wyckoff?"

"Usual investigation techniques and some instinct. I already knew Wyckoff had been working with Monk. I also recollected Wyckoff had a sister who ran off with a trucker. Before I left Fort Wayne, I went down to the PD to look up some records and found his name was Slack. I hunted him up when I got to Cleveland. They'd already been married and divorced, but he knew where Bobbie's living now. I went there and found Wyckoff."

I should have expected no less. There was too much bedrock cop under his bulk for him to overlook any obvious leads.

He asked, "Where did you find Gault?"

The question rocked me more than mine had rocked him. "At Arlene's place in Cincinnati. The trouble is, he's stashed Brandon somewhere. Do you have any ideas?"

"Here or Cincinnati?"

I gave him what some people like to call a Gallic shrug. "You tell me."

"Put a tail on him. Sooner or later he'll lead you to the kid." He had analyzed the problem and come up with the solution that could upset my plans for Brandon's safety.

"Not me. I don't have the time and I hate tail jobs. You're always at the mercy of the other person, going where he wants to go."

"Maybe I can find somebody. What did you find out about Tricia's murder?"

"It's a toss-up. I have some ideas about the way it might have happened, but even if I could prove it was murder, I still can't show Gault did it."

"We need to talk to Brandon." Hammond slapped his palm on the table, making plates jump. "The boy knows something."

"You hope he does. I hope it's not wishful thinking." I slid out of the booth, scooping up the check. "Stay in touch while I keep digging."

When I had paid for the meals, I went out to my car. Last night's rain had left puddles standing in the streets. Now that the sun was beating down on them, the water was evaporating into a muggy atmosphere. Instead of cooling things off, the rain was contributing to the stifling heat.

I drove down to Carnegie and across the Hope Memorial Bridge into Ohio City. In the early 1800s, that had been an entirely separate community on the west bank of the Cuyahoga River. It had been absorbed into Cleveland only after conditions had come to a near-pitched battle. Ohio City had finally capitulated, but it had never given up. Even a glance at the map shows that the streets of Ohio City don't blend into the Cleveland grid pattern. After lying low for a century and a half, Ohio City got its revenge in the last decade when the Yuppies seized upon it as an area for gentrification. Helen had invested money from her divorce settlement into the house on Bridge Avenue. Later, when we had started living together, she had put me to work refurbishing it. Because the brick outside had been basically sound, our efforts had been devoted to the inside. I had built new kitchen cabinets, I had drywalled the bedrooms, we had stripped off wallpaper downstairs and redone the woodwork.

Seeing the place now as I came down the street, I was thinking about the outside. Helen had been in favor of whitewashing the brick until I convinced her of the illogic of the move. Brick requires only minimal maintenance. If you are going to paint it, you might as well live in a frame house. I was campaigning to redo the windows to cut down on the heating bills, but the project on my mind was repairing the roof. We had already bought the shingles and were waiting only for a few consecutive days of clear weather when I could take off the time to do it. All these matters were much on my mind as I turned into Helen's driveway and parked in back. I was so absorbed I almost failed to see Helen, still in her robe, sitting on the back patio with the Sunday paper spread around. It took me even longer to realize we had company.

"Glad to see you're not resting on Sunday either," Manny Agosta told me as I came up. He was sitting at the redwood picnic table drinking coffee, wearing his sports jacket despite the heat, a sign he needed to cover up the sidearm on his hip. That meant he was on duty.

"Let me get some java, and I'll join you." I bent over to give Helen a kiss and went into the house as far as the kitchen, trying to think of all the implications of a visit by an on-duty Homicide dick. When I had poured my coffee, I came back. "Thought you had enough seniority to avoid weekend work."

"Vacation season. I have to fill in for the other guys until my turn comes up." Agosta looked into his cup as if he expected to see his vacation schedule posted there. He was having trouble broaching the subject that had brought him here.

I made it easy for him. "Ever turn anything on that body I found the other day?"

He looked up, grateful for a wedge into the subject. "One break. A motel on Brookpark complained about a car with Indiana plates in its lot. Turns out that car, a Lincoln, belongs to John Monk. He had been registered at the motel for a week before."

I ran my finger over my mustache. "If he had a motel room, what was he doing in the apartment?"

"That's why they call them mysteries." Agosta looked uncomfortably at Helen, who was lighting a cigarette while listening, then back at me. "We also found something else this morning. Some kids were playing around a garage on Lorain. They found the door unlocked and went inside.

Then they found a man in there, crushed under a car that had fallen on him."

"How awful for those kids!" Helen said.

"Guy's name was Ted Wyckoff, same one that rented the apartment where John Monk died."

"Son of a bitch," I said. "That a fact?"

Agosta showed me his impassive Aztec face. "I don't like it. People die all the time in accidents, but they aren't suspects in a homicide investigation. Something doesn't ring true."

"What are you hinting at, Manny? That Wyckoff was murdered?"

"It could be."

"Then you've got my sympathy because I wouldn't want to be in your shoes when you have to bring in the guy who picked up the car and dropped it on him."

Inside the house the phone rang. Helen got up to answer it.

"That isn't the way it happened," Agosta explained. "Wyckoff was working on a car that was being held up by a hook. Either the winch slipped or somebody let it go."

"Gil, it's for you," Helen called from the house.

Leaving Agosta with his bad humor for company, I went into the house and found Helen holding her hand over the mouthpiece. "It's Monica," she whispered. I took the receiver from her and spoke into it.

Monica said, "You better get over here right away."

"What happened?" Visions of Hammond somehow getting to Monica were flashing through my mind like scenes from an MTV video.

"Brandon. He's—he's started talking already. It would be best if you heard it firsthand."

"I'll get there as fast as I can. I've got problems on this end."

We hung up and I returned to Agosta at the picnic table. Helen stood aside watching us both, torn between hearing what Agosta had to say and finding out what Monica had wanted.

"We go back a long time," Agosta told me. "It's why I don't mind cutting some slack for you. At the same time, I trust you, Gil, not to pull any shenanigans with me or withhold any evidence. It's a contract between us, a working agreement, even if it's not in writing."

I nodded. "You can always count on me to hold up my end."

"Yeah. Except when you try to play games with me. Like this case. There's connections here I don't see. I hope to God you don't know anything I should. If you do, now's the time to tell me about it."

In other circumstances I might have taken him up on the offer, but I wasn't about to take the time with Monica's summons tugging at me. "I'm not holding out. I've been out of town the last couple days. If you want to check that, call Sergeant Gilmore in Cincinnati Homicide. I was talking to him around noon Friday."

"What were you doing there?"

"The child-snatching case I told you about. I got it settled."

"The same one Monk was connected with?"

"The same." We played the eyeball-to-eyeball game.

"You won't talk about it, I suppose," he said at last.

"All it takes is a subpoena to the grand jury."

"All right, Gil, it's your choice. Anything comes of it, we're cop and citizen."

"The only way I'd have it."

Agosta left a quarter inch of coffee in his cup when he started back to the street where his car was parked. I felt a door had closed between us that would be hard to open again. When I turned around, Helen was studying me with suspicion.

"Ted Wyckoff was the man you went looking for last

night. He was also the man you roughed up when I was with you."

I nodded. "Is that a question?"

She asked it with gritted teeth. "You didn't tamper with any evidence?"

"I found his body. I just didn't report it." I waited to see if she wanted any further explanations before I added, "You'd better get dressed. Monica has learned something from Brandon."

23

WHEN MONICA OPENED THE DOOR, her eyes slid off my shoulder to Helen standing by my side. "You came, too. Good."

That was as much as we got in the way of a greeting. She turned and walked back inside her apartment, leaving the door open. It was up to us if we wanted to enter. I looked at Helen, shrugged, and let her precede me over the threshold.

Monica had crossed the living room into her kitchen where she was packing pop cans in a Styrofoam ice chest. "This apartment is not very large," she explained. "I'm going to take Brandon on a picnic."

"Nice day for it," I said, not sure what kind of response I should give.

A toilet flushed and soon Brandon came into the living room. He was not exactly running and skipping, but he was not moving at the same lethargic pace I had seen in Fort Wayne. "I'm ready, Miss Brodbeck," he announced. He was wearing a T-shirt and jeans, his ball cap on his head. He had his glove and a scuffed baseball with him. "Are you going to bring your glove?"

"My brother's glove. He gave it to me when I was playing on a softball team. But yes, I'll bring it if you want."

"I know you." Brandon was looking at me. "You came to my game and you talked to Grandpa and you helped Aunt Arlene when Grandma was yelling at her."

"I'm the one," I admitted.

"Brandon," Monica said, nodding to Helen, "could you show this lady where my car is? She could help you carry our picnic supplies down. We'll get started that much faster."

"Sure he can." Helen took the hint and picked up the ice chest. "My name is Helen, Brandon."

Monica gave her keys to Brandon, who carried the picnic basket as they went out. When the two of them were gone, I asked, "What happened?"

"Brandon had a nightmare last night. Afterwards, I sat with him in my lap and it all came gushing out. Can't you see he's been through a catharsis?"

"There's been a change all right."

"Arlene did it. She killed Tricia."

Somehow I wasn't ready to accept Arlene's guilt too quickly when Monica had been doing the questioning. "He said it was Arlene?"

"Not in so many words." Monica was impatient with my skepticism. "If you don't believe me, you can ask him yourself."

"I will, if the opportunity arises. What did he tell you?"

"That he came home from school and let himself in. That he looked all over the house for his mother. He heard some-one moving around but he couldn't see them. He went down in the basement and found his mother's body. Then he heard a door slam and ran upstairs, but the person was gone."

"That's all?" It was the first confirmation that someone besides Tricia had been in the house, but it didn't make the mystery person Arlene.

"Brandon remembers seeing a purse in the house when he first came in. It was gone when he went back upstairs. Ar-lene's purse."

I said, "We had better catch up with the others."

Helen and I followed Monica's Honda the short distance to the Rocky River Reservation, proving once again the fallacy of small cars being a solution to the gas crisis. With Monica, Brandon, and the picnic supplies in the Honda, there had been no room for Helen and me. At least the separation gave me a chance to bring Helen up to date on what Monica had discovered.

"Can you be sure Monica didn't plant the idea?" Helen asked, this suggestion coming from the woman who accuses me of being a cynic for doubting the testimony of children every time the news carries a story of mass molestation at a day school.

"I'll try to check it out."

The Rocky River Reservation is part of the Cleveland Metroparks, essentially a series of recreation areas along the banks of the rivers in the area. A road winds through the valley vaguely parallel to the river course through woods growing more or less wild up the valley walls. At intervals there are areas with picnic tables and swing sets just off the road on patches of level bottomland. Monica turned into one of them that was not being used.

Brandon explored to the edge of the clearing, while I helped the two women set up the table. When he had seen as much as he wanted, Brandon came to me to ask if I wanted to play catch. Monica gave me her glove, a much-used fielder's model whose original color had faded to blond, and I took Brandon over to a level open spot to loosen up. Standing forty feet away, I lobbed easy ones to him. He snagged the majority of them without trouble and burned throws back to me. Even after I was sure he could handle hard throws, I kept lobbing out of respect for my own unconditioned arm. Brandon grew impatient with me, zinging one down by my shoelaces and the next over my head where I had to leap for it. He showed surprise that I didn't let either of them get by me.

"Let's try some tough ones." I backed up and threw a pop-up for him. He took two steps to his right and pulled it in, a long way from the inept player I had watched only three days ago. He threw some high ones to me, making me run way up or back. I did the same to him, but with less distance for him to move. A few experiments soon showed me his problem, hardly unique, was handling those he had to go back on.

"Don't back-pedal," I told him. "Turn around and surround it. Get in front of it so it's going to come down on your nose, but for God's sake, don't forget to put your glove up."

Brandon listened to my advice and watched my demonstrations, soon getting the idea. When he was catching more than he missed, I switched to grounders and discovered another problem. Instead of getting in front of the ball, he tried to run alongside it and spear it with his glove. I showed him how to get in front of it and go down on one knee to keep the ball from going through his legs. Given a whole weekend, I might have turned him into the best fielder in his division. Of course, I would have given out first. I called a halt and flopped down in the shade.

"Boy, you sure know how to play baseball!" Brandon said, settling down beside me. It was good to see him showing enthusiasm for something.

"If I'm so great, why is it I'm not playing shortstop for the New York Yankees?"

"Why not?" he asked innocently.

"Because I could never hit an outside curve," I told him.

"Bet you could hit it way over the fence," he insisted.

"Not against Big League pitching. Not against minor leagues, either." I pushed myself up against a tree and reached for my Camels. "Brandon, I want to talk about some of the things that have been happening to you. Do you want to talk about them?"

"I guess." He pounded the ball into his glove.

"Part of it is what you told Miss Brodbeck last night, about the day your mother died. You said you saw a purse in your house, a purse that didn't belong there. Is that right?"

"Uh-huh." *Thunk!* went the ball into the web.

"Where was it?"

"On the chair."

"What chair?"

"By the desk."

"The writing desk?"

"Uh-huh."

He was backsliding on me, retreating into his private cocoon. I wished I knew how far to press him. "Tell me more about the purse and then we can forget it."

"It was a big purse and it had a strap on it to go clear up here." He pointed to his shoulder. "It had lots of pockets in it, for different things."

"What color was it?"

Brandon looked around as if he were trying to find an object of the right color. He picked up the glove I had been using. "Like that."

"Tan? Beige?" My suggestions drew nods from Brandon. I tried the one I had to ask. "Do you know anyone who carries a purse like that?"

"Aunt Arlene."

I had to agree with him. I had seen it the night I was in Fort Wayne when she may have used it to signal Gault.

"And it had a box in it," Brandon added.

"You looked inside?"

He shook his head. "I could see it, the shape of it."

"How big a box?"

He showed me with his hands. "Like a box of candy."

It made no sense that I could see, but I filed it away. I realized I had been holding an unlit cigarette, so I took care of that, puffing away while I gave Brandon a break. He stood up and threw the ball high in the air and then got under it, waiting for it to come down. At the last second he put his glove up and caught it.

"See?" he said proudly. "It was coming right for my nose."

"You learn fast," I told him. "It's a good idea to have a glove with strips of leather in the webbing. That way you can look through the web at the coming ball. You can't do that if your web is solid."

Brandon examined his glove to see that it had the right kind of web.

"Could you answer some more questions?" I asked.

"What about?"

"The man who kidnapped you on the way to practice."

"I didn't like that. It was bad until Grandpa and Grandma came to rescue me."

"Bad how?"

"Bad touching. There's good touching and bad touching. The man hurt me." Brandon dropped down onto his knees. "He asked me all kinds of questions about Mommy. Not like you did. He got mean and yelled at me, and when I didn't answer the right right way, he told me God would punish me. He hit me, too. And he made me go to the bedroom. Later on, he came in the bedroom and started the bad touching. It hurt me. I stayed in the bedroom and cried a lot."

"Did you tell him about Aunt Arlene's purse?"

"Yes."

"Did you see his gun?"

"He had it on his belt, like policemen on TV. Then he took it off and put it on a shelf where I couldn't reach it. That was before he started asking me questions."

"What happened to the man?"

Brandon shrugged.

"Did the gun shoot him?"

"I guess. There was a big noise."

"Who was holding the gun?"

"I don't know. I was in the bedroom. I stayed there and cried a lot. I didn't want him to come in and hurt me again."

"Did you ever go into the bathroom?"

"When I had to go to the toilet. It hurt to poopie."

"Did you ever hold the gun?"

"It was up on a shelf. I couldn't reach it."

I studied Brandon, wondering if he were lying deliberately, or if he had blocked his memory so well he had no recall of even peripheral details, like what room he had been in. "Where were you when your Grandpa found you?"

"In the bedroom."

"Not in the bathroom?"

Brandon shook his head.

Except I knew from Hammond's account that Brandon had been hiding in the bathtub with the Cobra lying on the bathroom floor. I tried a different angle. "Who do you think killed the man?"

"God killed him. That's what Grandma said. It was God's punishment. When Grandpa carried me out of the bedroom, Grandma was reading to the dead man from the Bible."

"Did you see the gun?"

"It was on the floor by the dead man's chair."

The women were still over by the picnic table, watching Brandon and me in the shade. I flipped my cigarette away and patted Brandon's knee. "We'd better go eat now. Can't keep the ladies waiting."

The picnic meal we ate was desultory for the adults. I suppose the food was all right, although my idea of a summer meal always seems to be located in an air-conditioned restaurant where you don't have to share it with flies. Brandon didn't mind. He had to tell Monica and Helen what he had learned about going down on one knee for a grounder and how to catch a fly ball looking through the web. Fearful they weren't showing enough interest, he repeated it a few more times to make sure no one missed the point. He had no problem being excused to go play on the swing set.

I gathered up the disposable items and dumped them in a trash can, while Helen helped Monica pack leftovers away. When I came back, I fished a can of Classic Coke out of the ice chest, pulled the ring tab, and sat down to drink it. Folding the red checked tablecloth, Helen watched Brandon swinging.

"He's anything but catatonic now," she observed. "You've done wonders, Monica."

Monica closed the lid on the picnic basket. "I wasn't playing catch with him. It sounds as if he learned all there is to know about baseball."

I shrugged modestly and sipped my Coke.

"So what did you learn out there?" Monica asked, looking at me with her strangely oblique gaze.

"It was Arlene's purse. It doesn't add up the way I had it figured, but there you are." I drank more Coke and tried to deny what was in front of me. "For a while, I thought I had it doped out so I could explain what happened to Tricia and get Brandon off the hook for Monk's murder. I guess you can't have everything."

"Then Brandon really did shoot the Monk?" Helen asked.

"The story he tells just doesn't fit the known facts. My guess is that he's developed a form of amnesia covering the time around the shooting. Yet he understands what happened to him as far as the molesting goes."

"Understandable," Monica judged. "Consider the traumas he's been through this last year."

I finished my Coke and crushed the can. "How would it be if you give Helen a ride home? When we leave here, I have an errand to run."

Monica nodded. "Of course."

I flipped my empty Coke can into the trash container with a hook shot and called to Brandon: "Ready for some more?"

Brandon jumped off the swing and grabbed his glove as I trotted back to our playing field.

24

WHEN I EMERGED from the Rocky River Reservation onto Sloane Avenue in Lakewood, I stopped at the first pay phone to call ahead to Arlene's apartment to let her know I was coming. Then I drove on to Clifton and cruised down to the block I wanted. Early dusk settling in on a Sunday evening reminded me that I was missing "60 Minutes." Ahead I recognized the apartment building and turned up a side street to find a parking space.

I hiked back around the corner and up the walk to the mailbox alcove and punched the Hrnailovich bell. The electronic version of Arlene's voice asked who it was and I said, "Disbro." The door buzzer sounded and I pushed it open as something moved behind me and something hard pushed into my kidney.

A voice above and behind my left ear said, "Just keep moving."

Once through the security door, I looked over my shoulder to see Wes Hammond standing there with his .45 pointed at me. "We're going up to Arlene's apartment together," he informed me and pushed my face against the wall while his free hand frisked me.

"What's that going to accomplish?"

"Everything." Hammond's one-hand search was quick and efficient, satisfying him that I was unarmed. "Go ahead."

I punched the elevator button and while we waited, I asked conversationally, "Where were you hiding?"

"Across the street where I could watch this building. When I saw you coming, I hurried up behind you. You should be more careful of your backside."

"I should do a lot of things different."

When the elevator arrived empty, I got on first. Hammond followed, keeping as far away from me as the tiny car allowed, holding his pistol tight against his side with his body turned away from me so I couldn't grab for it with any reasonable hope of success. I didn't need that. I needed a TV villain who would offer the gun for easy taking. I was facing front; Hammond, back. He reached out and pressed the button for 3.

We rode that way until the elevator stopped and the door slid open. Hammond jerked his head to order me out, a gesture that was strictly George Raft. I obeyed it anyway, moving reluctantly toward Arlene's door. There, he positioned himself on the hinge side, holding his gun in a two-handed grip with the muzzle down, the way he had done it the night at my motel room. He gave me another George Raft nod, this time meaning for me to knock.

She must have been waiting on the other side of the door.

It opened as if my knuckles had touched a magic spring. Before I could shake my head, she said, "Come in, Gil."

As I started to enter, Hammond pushed me from behind, propelling me into Arlene and forcing her to stagger backwards. We danced into the room locked in a weird tango. Hammond followed and shut the door. Arlene's eyes told me the instant when she recognized him.

"Where's Gault?" Hammond demanded through clenched teeth when he didn't see him in the living room.

"Not here." Arlene was pressed tight against me as I held her up. She found her balance and stepped away from me, her eyes apportioning guilt in my direction. "How did this happen?"

"Sorry. He waylaid me downstairs."

Not taking his daughter's word, Hammond moved through the apartment looking into the other rooms. Satisfied at last, he came back to us in the living room that was furnished with the equipment from defunct companies. "Where is he?"

"Go to hell," Arlene said.

Hammond took it with more sorrow than anger. "Don't be that way, Arlene. It doesn't gain you anything in the long run."

"What will you do? Beat me?" She was standing with her arms tight at her sides, defying him.

"You know I won't. I'm your father." Despite his words, Hammond's voice hummed with his conflicting loyalties. Pressures from his wife were doing battle with his love for his daughter and his decades of training in law enforcement. His pent-up frustrations were making him dangerous, maybe more volatile than Arlene realized.

"Then be my father. Don't be Mom's hired hand."

"I can't go back now." The words had a finality to them as

if he were playing out a script written long ago. "And don't ask that of me. I've been married to Esther longer than you've been alive."

"Oh, Dad!" The words summed up Arlene's lifetime of frustration.

"Anyway, I don't want Gault. It's Brandon I came for."

"He isn't here, either."

"But you'll tell me where he is."

"If you can't beat me, what do you think is going to make me?"

Hammond raised the muzzle of his .45 to my chest. "If you don't, I'll shoot him."

Letting a family argument run its course while I stood on the sidelines had seemed like good advice, which for once in my life I had been following. Look where it got me.

Arlene studied her father as if gauging his seriousness, swiveled her head my direction, then looked back at him. She opened her mouth to say something but clamped it tightly shut as she changed her mind.

"Guess you're going to have to shoot," I told Hammond.

"Guess so." His thumb pushed down the safety with a distinct click that seemed as loud to me as a crash of cymbals.

I asked, trying not to sound desperate, "Then what will you do about Arlene? Leave her alive to testify against you? She will, you know. If she does, you'll go to prison for a long time. Then what happens to Brandon? So if you want Brandon like you claim, you're going to kill Arlene in addition to me. Are you up to that?"

Hammond didn't lower his pistol, an omen to which I attached malevolent implications.

"How about it, Dad? Will you kill me? Will you shoot the daughter you won't strike?"

Staring down the muzzle of the .45 like the guest of honor

at a firing squad, I reached for a cigarette. Hell, I had earned it. "Go ahead, Hammond," I invited without putting my heart into it. "Shit or get off the pot."

All he had to do was pull the trigger. All that stood in his way was a lifetime devoted to law and order. Seconds ticked by with the speed of hardening cement while I waited to see which way he would tilt, unsure of the outcome. When the time comes for jumping the rails, no one does it as thoroughly as a cop or with as large a propensity for violence. For them a small step across the line is a gigantic leap to the far side, maybe because they recognize no degrees of the evil they have been fighting. Jaywalking or mass murder—once the line is transgressed, you might as well go all the way. Hammond's eyes told me he was poised there, ready for the big leap. At last he pushed the safety up with a click that didn't seem as loud as the last one. He put the pistol in a holster on his right hip under his coat.

"Him I could shoot, but not you." Hammond showed his defeat in the slump of his shoulders. He went back to the door, pausing with his hand on the knob. "Sure you don't want to tell me, Arlene? It could save Gault's life when I find him."

She shook her head in the Hammond gesture of denial. "Don't, Dad."

He opened the door and went out into the hall. I stood watching until he got on the elevator and the doors closed. Only then did I shut Arlene's door and turn back to her. She exhaled a long stream of breath and went into the kitchen where she took down a bottle of scotch from a shelf and poured some into a glass. She drank half of it in one sip and closed her eyes, waiting for the burn to subside. When she opened them again, she found me watching her while I lit my cigarette with unsteady fingers.

"Where is Gault, anyway?" I asked.

"He went to his house to pick up some books and papers for his research project." She finished off the scotch in the glass. "Have you learned anything from Brandon?"

The question reminded me of the reason for coming here. I inhaled a deep lungful of smoke to make the transition to the new topic. "Enough to establish that Tricia was murdered."

Arlene looked up from pouring herself a second drink. "Do you have any idea who did it?"

"Her sister."

My choice of words created a delay in Arlene's reaction while she parsed the meaning. "You're accusing me?"

I gave her credit for the control she showed over her emotions. "I can even tell you how it came about. You went to your sister's house for an afternoon visit. You walked in and found her note on the writing desk. You read it and thought it was a suicide note. You dropped your purse on the chair. You went running through the house thinking you were going to find her body. Surprise. You found her in the laundry room, doing the wash. Not only was she alive, she was happy. She was leaving to start a new life. She probably told you about it, confessed she was a lesbian."

Arlene had been shaking her head at virtually every word I uttered. "None of this ever happened. None of it."

"About this time the idea hit you. If you had thought Tricia's farewell was a suicide note, so would other people, provided she was found dead in the right circumstances. You grabbed the nearest weapon, something from the laundry, and strangled her until she collapsed. Then you put her head in the noose to finish the job—but we've already covered that."

"My sister? Why would I want to kill her?"

"For Gault."

"But she was leaving Alan. She was getting out of his life, leaving me what I wanted. Even if I had been there, there would have been no purpose in killing her at that point."

She was convincing—so convincing I had to muffle my ears to what she was saying. "Maybe you wanted to protect Alan from scandal. How do I know what resentments had built up between sisters over the years? Men have been known to kill because their neighbor's dog ordered it. Maybe you were hearing voices."

"Listen to me, please," Arlene said tightly, her voice ready to slip into anger. "I wasn't there and I didn't do it. When Tricia died I was at WLW studios having an important meeting with the station management and some key sponsors. The meeting started at ten o'clock and we were still at it when my office called to tell me Tricia was dead. At no time was I out of sight of at least four or five people. I couldn't have done it."

"Alibis can be broken," I said. "The reason yours has held up is that it hasn't been tested because everyone was thinking suicide. Now that it's murder, your alibi will crumble apart when the police look into it."

"It will not. It's the truth."

"Arlene, I know it's a lie. I know you were in the house when Brandon came home. He saw your purse on the chair by the writing table. He even saw the outline of the box you had inside."

Arlene's brow wrinkled. "What purse?"

I grabbed her wrist then and pulled her out of the kitchen, across the living room, into her bedroom. I flipped on the light, opened the closet door, and rummaged around until I found the right purse. I turned and shoved it into her stomach like a medicine ball. "That one."

I must have shoved harder than I intended, because Arlene backed into the bed and sat down hard on it, the purse landing in her lap. She looked down at it. "This purse? It was part of a set, with a couple pieces of overnight luggage. The maker was a sponsor at one of the Cincinnati stations." She picked it up and thrust it back at me. "This is not the only purse of its kind in the world. I had two sets. Gil, I gave one of them away."

The purse was there only inches away from my face. I narrowed my focus on it, ignoring Arlene. Synapses were popping in my mind, racing through syllogisms of logic. Without asking, I knew the name of the person who had received the second purse as surely as I knew that Arlene was telling the truth.

"My God!" In that instant of clarity, she had seen the same thing I had. A noise came from deep in her throat, somewhere between a cough and retching as she faced the truth. "No," she said in a low voice that stretched the single word into a moan.

But it was beyond any denial. Maybe I had accepted it a little faster than she had. Already I was jumping ahead to other subjects, other deaths.

"No, no, no," Arlene repeated, shaking her head in the Hammond manner.

"Face it," I told her. "It's time we did something about it."

25

MY DRIVE ACROSS CLEVELAND that night was a contest to see how many laws I could violate. On the Shoreway I was less of a menace than upon the surface streets but still no model of rational action. I wove through the traffic that was doing a mere seventy, switching lanes without regard for anybody who might have claimed a superior right to the road, slamming on my brakes as I drew too close to a new set of taillights. In the passenger seat Arlene held tight to whatever she could find and watched the blur of passing scenery.

Liberty Boulevard would have been my natural exit, but it had changed its name and been closed for repairs. I went on to Eddy Road and turned off into neighborhoods you wouldn't want to traverse in daylight. On a hot Sunday night, the people who lived there had come out of their stifling homes and apartments to sit on the stoop or in their yards to drink beer and yell across at their neighbors. We crossed the line into East Cleveland, a suburb unlike any other in the world with the possible exception of Soweto. Cadillacs and Lincolns, Volvos and Mercedes, on their way to the affluent homes in the adjoining suburbs, passed like burning matches being waved over a gasoline spill.

No matter how I hurried, the car lagged behind the pace of my thoughts. While Arlene sat quiet, I scanned the data collected in my mind to sort out the facts I needed. Half an hour ago in Arlene's apartment, I'd had nothing but a sudden insight that gave me a wedge into the answers I had been looking for. Now I was filling in the steps I had leaped over, making sure they led logically to the right conclusion, testing them to be positive there was no other direction they could take.

As soon as Hammond had left, Arlene tried calling Gault only to get no answer. Either his phone was unplugged, or he simply wasn't answering. We had to assume Hammond was headed for Gault's house. If we were wrong, no harm was done. If we were right, we were on the brink of another killing.

We zigzagged around the Forest Hills Shopping Mall and followed Superior into Cleveland Heights, where I turned onto Gault's street and then into his driveway. Lights were on in the house and a Jeep Wagoneer with Indiana plates sat in his driveway. Arlene had her door open while I was still braking the Chevy, and by the time I had stepped out, she was already through the front door of Gault's house. Instead of rushing after her, I went to the trunk and got out the .38 snub nose that had been concealed there for most of the week and carried it over to the Jeep. Hammond had been too

hasty getting out of it to lock the doors behind him. I opened
the one on the passenger side and slipped the .38 under the
seat. Back at my still-open trunk, I fished out my own piece, a
Smith & Wesson Model 19 with a four-inch barrel that had
once been my service revolver. Sticking it in the waistband of
my jeans, I followed Arlene to the house.

The door stood ajar after her entrance. I pushed through it
and followed the sound of voices into the living room where
Tricia's pastel portrait looked down on the people grouped
at her feet. Gault stood at one side with Arlene gripping his
arm. They made one point of a triangle with the other points
formed by Hammond and his wife spaced wide apart. Esther
had her hands folded and her head inclined forward. Hammond held the same .45 he had pointed at me earlier.

"Drop it, Hammond," I ordered.

He looked over his shoulder and saw me in the doorway,
bracing my two-hand grip against the frame so that little
more than my right eye was exposed sighting over my Smith.
"Sure you can drop the hammer?" he asked.

"Absolutely."

My voice must have sounded more convincing to him
than it did to me. He let his Commander thud onto the thick
carpet as if he were releasing his grip on life.

"Step away from it."

When he obeyed, I exposed myself to enter the room and
pick it up. I stuck it in my hip pocket and put my own
weapon away. "There, isn't that more sociable?" I asked.

Suddenly no one wanted to comment. I turned to Gault.
"What have I missed?"

"They want Brandon. He was threatening me with expos-
ing Brandon as a killer unless I gave him up." Gault's gaze
fell from mine. "I was about to agree."

"Don't sweat it," I told him. "Hammond spread that
murder story to me hoping I would pass it on to you. Which

I did. Once that was done, we were all caught up in a conspiracy of silence that would have kept us from asking what really happened in the apartment with Monk."

"The boy has no guilt," Esther assured us. "He was possessed by evil forces when he fired the shot."

"Except he didn't fire any shot," I said.

"Are you saying Monk killed himself after all?" Gault asked.

"It was murder, all right, but not by Brandon."

Arlene turned her head toward her father. "Dad? You didn't!"

Hammond stood mute. When I saw he was doing nothing to defend himself, I spoke up. "If he had wanted to kill Monk and rig a suicide, he could have done a better job of it. He was stuck working with what he had, covering up what had already been done. He framed Brandon because he was protecting someone else."

"Who?" Arlene asked in confusion.

"He was an evil man," Esther said, all eyes suddenly on her. "What he had done to the child was unspeakable. We found Brandon in a terrible state. The evidence was plain."

"Shut up, Esther," Hammond advised. "Don't say anything."

"The gun was there on the shelf in its holster. Monk mocked me when I accused him. I realized then that God had placed the gun there for my use. I grabbed it. The evil one was laughing right up to the instant the noise of the shot drowned it out."

"Where was your husband?"

"In the bedroom, ministering to Brandon."

"When he heard the shot, he must have come running out. Where were you by that time?"

"Away from John Monk. I had done my duty and walked away. I don't remember it all clearly."

"And dropped the gun on the floor across the room?"

Esther breathed heavily with her efforts to recall. "I simply don't know for certain."

Hammond was not about to help out. Too many years of police experience had taught him not to talk. I addressed myself to Esther. "You see, I knew all along that Brandon never fired that gun. The holster was on a shelf too high for him to reach. That's what led me to think of someone else, of you, because God has given you the sign to kill before. Isn't that the way it worked with Tricia?"

Esther's eyes focused on mine for a few seconds and then shifted to the portrait of her daughter. "The Lord often works in mysterious ways. He was directing me the day I went to their home in Cincinnati early and found Tricia in bed with her neighbor. Sin! With a man it would have been venal enough. But with another woman!"

"Like the farewell note she had written. You found that note on the writing desk one day when you dropped in to see her. You had a habit of doing that unexpectedly. As soon as you saw the note, you knew what it meant. You realized Tricia had gone back to her lesbian ways."

"She swore to me that was all behind her. I prayed for her soul and I thought she had mended her ways," Esther explained. "When I saw that note I knew God had not answered my prayers. Evil had gripped her as surely as it has gripped Arlene. If Tricia had lived another ten years, it would have been ten years of sin she would have to account for. Better she should die early with a soul less stained. I understood then what He wanted me to do."

"You found Tricia in the basement doing the laundry. You confronted her, the two of you argued, you yanked something out of the laundry basket and strangled her."

Esther's hand went to her throat. "My scarf. It was a raw day and I had a wool scarf under my coat. I used that."

So much for all my deductions from the laundry basket. At least it had put me on the right track. "After Tricia collapsed, you put her in the noose. Was that from things your husband had told you?"

"Wesley had talked about such things. I had seen illustrations in his textbooks, so I knew the body did not have to swing free. These things came back to me as I realized the note upstairs could be read as a suicide note. Let everyone be misled. God and I would know the truth."

"Jesus!" All heads in the room turned to find the source of the voice. It had come from Hammond. "Your own daughter? You never told me about that. And then you set me to hounding Gault?"

"He is guilty enough for his many sins. What does it matter if he was hounded for this one or another?" Esther's reasoning would have made her dean of philosophy at the Inquisition. "Is what I did any worse that what you did to Brandon?"

"Yes," he answered quickly, "because you made everything else necessary."

"No," she countered. "We had to rescue Brandon anyway."

I butted into their discussion. "Speaking of Brandon, he came home while you were still in the basement. He saw your purse when he came in. He even saw the shape of a box through the material. At least Brandon thought it was a box. I imagine it was your Bible. He went looking for his mother. You sneaked up to the main floor and hid out. Brandon came downstairs and headed for the basement. You grabbed your purse and ran out while Brandon was discovering the body.

"Later, during the investigation and the funeral, you took care of Brandon for a few days. It gave you a chance to find out exactly what he knew. You had him draw pictures to learn he had known there was a third person in the house.

Brandon depicted the third person as a man, even though he should have suspected it was a woman after seeing the purse. Your influence was probably responsible for that. When the subject of the purse did come up, you made sure he remembered Arlene had one like that. She did, but it was part of a pair, the other one of which she had given you. If Brandon ever knew that, you made sure he forgot. If you had any smarts, you chucked your purse out as soon as you could."

All this talk had left my throat parched. I would have gone for a drink of water if I could have trusted the group together while I was gone. I settled for licking my lips.

Gault had been standing for all this with Arlene still clutching his arm. He pulled away from her gently and made for a chair. "It's all over then. No more running and hiding."

"No more running and hiding," I assured him, "but it's not over yet. We still have one more death to account for. Ted Wyckoff is no longer with us."

Arlene followed Gault to the chair and sat on the arm and began kneading his shoulders. She looked at her mother who was standing apart now, holding herself rigid. No earthly judgment would ever affect her. "Does she get credit for another one?" Arlene asked.

I answered by speaking to Esther. "You get the credit, right? You went after him because of the gun that killed Monk. You arrived in Cleveland two days ago and learned the police were treating Monk's death as a murder. All you needed was to read the newspapers for the last few days. It was enough to tell you the gun had not been found in the apartment. You figured Wyckoff had taken it out."

"He told us a lie. He said his sister had removed the gun and then given it to some man she didn't know."

I nodded. "Obviously. Was that any reason to kill him?"

"I didn't kill him," Esther maintained. "The hand of God struck him down."

"That's wearing a little thin," I said.

"It's the truth. After Wesley had talked to him, he called the motel. Wesley was out looking for Gault. I talked to Mr. Wyckoff who wanted to meet with me. He arranged to be at Ernie's Garage. I took a taxi there and found him working under his car. He had been doing some thinking, he said. If Wesley and I knew the gun should have been in the apartment, we must have guilty knowledge of the crime. Wyckoff was convinced my husband had killed Monk. He wanted money to keep quiet. He didn't call it blackmail. He said he would work to earn it, by trying to recover the gun and help us find Brandon. The whole business overwhelmed me. I felt faint and leaned against the wall. Suddenly the car that Mr. Wyckoff was working under crashed down on him. Later, I realized I must have touched the handle. God ushered me into it."

"Not this time," I said levelly. "I think you deliberately flipped that switch. The reason you paid Wyckoff for that gun and then dropped the car on him was so you could take your money back off his body."

"That simply isn't so."

"Then how did you come to have the gun?"

"That isn't possible," Hammond said, his eyes narrowing suspiciously.

I jerked my head to Gault. "Go out and look in their car. If you find a snub-nosed .38, don't touch it. I'll call the police and when they get here, you can swear out an affidavit that you saw it so they can get a search warrant and find it legally."

Gault got up from his chair, following my orders. Arlene studied her mother for a moment, then got up and put a hand on her shoulder. Esther reacted as if she had been touched by a live wire. Arlene said, "You must be very tired, Mom. Wouldn't you like to sit down and rest?"

"Yes, I am tired."

Arlene steered her over to the couch under Tricia's portrait. Esther sat and Arlene encouraged her to fall over sideways until her head rested on the pillow.

"You can be a thoughtful daughter, sometimes," Esther told her. "Why couldn't you have led a moral life? You could have been better than Tricia."

From across the room, Hammond said to me, "You'll never make this frame stick."

I shrugged. "It's a piece of hard evidence—the murder weapon in your possession. The police will be grateful enough they won't want to question it." I went across the room to pick up a telephone that I used to call the Cleveland Heights police and told them I was holding a homicide suspect who had confessed to two murders in Cleveland. They took down my name and the address and promised to be right over.

Finished with that call, I put another one through to Manny Agosta at home. I told him the same thing. He took it with poor grace, his voice nearly wrecking the instrument. He also promised to come over.

Before that night was through, I did more fast talking than I had ever done in my life.

26

I TOOK WEDNESDAY of that week as my day off because the weather reports were guaranteeing three consecutive days of sunshine. Helen had been after me to shingle the roof and this was my chance. While she taught her classes, I climbed to the roof and began tearing off the old shingles. Once that was done, I replaced boards where they were needed and stapled down a layer of tarpaper. I was still nailing rows of new shingles in place when Helen returned. Never one to trust a weatherman, not even one certified by the American Meteorological Association, I kept hammering away to get as much as possible accomplished while daylight lasted.

Thirty feet above street level, I saw the car approaching, saw it park, and saw her get out—but I kept working until

Helen notified me we had company. Only then did I climb down the ladder into the yard littered with scraps of old shingles and tarpaper. Monica Brodbeck was drinking lemonade with Helen at the picnic table on the patio.

"Excuse the mess," I apologized, not offering to shake hands in deference to the dirt on me.

"I see I could have picked a more convenient time to drop by," Monica noted. "I didn't mean to interrupt your work."

"You're doing me a favor. I'm overdue for a break." I went into the house to wash up a little. I also poured myself a cup of coffee and got my cigarettes, which I carried out to the women at the picnic table.

Monica looked at me with her disconcerting eyes. "You don't look much like a detective." She meant the clothes I wore—T-shirt, jeans, baseball cap with a Smith & Wesson logo on it, tool holster, and carpenter's apron. She wore the same dress as when she first came to my office, a week ago today.

"How is your star boarder?" I asked.

"Brandon went back to live with Professor Gault. He hopes you'll soon teach him how to bat."

"Maybe it could be arranged. Will you still be tutoring him?"

"I guess so. Right now we're taking a little vacation." She dropped her eyes to her hands folded on the picnic table, then raised them again to me. "Is it safe for him to be home?"

"Why not? Esther is in jail facing three counts of murder. Hammond is also out of the way, charged with kidnapping and accessory to murder. He might make bail eventually. I saw his application cross Gladys's desk at Moe Glickman's yesterday."

Monica looked out across Helen's back yard as if she could

see them in their cells, marking off days on a calendar. She turned back to me. "What will happen to them?"

"Hammond will do some time, how much depending on his degree of cooperation. The length of his sentence isn't so important. At his age, even a few years could be a life sentence."

"And his wife?"

That was a tougher prediction. "Three counts of murder, two of them in Cuyahoga County, are hard to beat. She will never get the death penalty, if that's your question. Even a first-year law student could figure out her best plea is insanity—at least diminished capacity. Most likely she won't even spend time in prison but in some kind of institution where she can read her Bible and pray all day. In a way, it will be the kind of life she longed for."

"You hear stories—is there a chance—she could be found not guilty?"

"Not very likely. Despite all the Miranda warnings, Esther copped out to the killings. She was bragging about what she had done, proud that God had chosen her as His instrument. Without that boasting, the evidence was pretty thin. She did the state a favor by taking the focus off whether she was guilty and placing it on her mental state. Yesterday a detective named Gilmore came up from Cincinnati to question her. She gave him a complete account of Tricia's murder down there. Even if she should beat the rap here, she would still have to face another murder charge in Hamilton County." I shook my head. "It's all over except for the legal processes running their course."

Helen had been watching me with an expression that dared me to bring up my part in planting the Cobra in Hammond's car. We had had some full and frank discussions, as the diplomats say, on that point. While Helen had maintained planting evidence is always a trifle illegal, I had pointed out that I had been restoring it. That little snub nose had traveled so far while others tried to remove it from the scene of the crime; I had merely put it back where it could implicate the person who, after all, was guilty. The importance of the murder weapon had been reduced to insignificance by Esther's ready confession. Helen had been slow to reduce my crime from a felony to a misdemeanor.

Monica had received the news she had come to hear. "It's over for Brandon now, too. He doesn't have to fear being hauled away in the middle of the night. He can concentrate on getting back to a normal life."

"Kids are pretty resilient," Helen put in. "At least now no one is messing with his mind. After a decent period, he can get back to thinking about baseball instead of killings."

"He still might need professional therapy," Monica said.

"Even so, it shouldn't take long," Helen assured her. "He'll come back."

I sipped my coffee and waited for Monica to say something more, maybe state the purpose of her visit. She began groping toward it: "I came simply to say thank you for all you have done. Now that I'm here, I'm having trouble coming up with adequate words. It seems so hollow."

"I managed to get Gault and Brandon back. I feel like I failed you in the rest."

Monica understood as she fixed that odd stare on me again. "Irony. It seems my efforts to get Alan back only drove him closer to Arlene. I wouldn't be surprised if those two get married one day. But that's exactly what you warned me about from the very start, isn't it?"

"Sort of."

"When you start out searching for the truth," Helen said, "you should be prepared for the day when the facts add up to something you don't want to know."

Monica finished her lemonade and made noises about leaving. Helen and I walked with her to the gate in the fence around the front yard, where she stopped and turned and planted a kiss on my cheek. "Maybe that's the word I was looking for." Monica turned quickly then and hurried off to her car.

When she had driven away, Helen and I walked back toward her house. I tried to slip my arm around her waist but she pushed me away. "You're filthy."

"That's because of the bitch I work for. She holds me in involuntary servitude and works me to death."

"I hear there are some very good fringe benefits."

"Only if I can collect them."

"Clean yourself up and we'll see about that."

I did, leaving my roofing job half-finished. An hour later, while I was in bed with Helen, the thunderclap announced the start of a summer downpour.

I never did trust weathermen.